Buried deep in the past is the key to peace...and a monstrous treachery

Earth faces total domination
by an alien force. The Galactic medallion,
the only key to freedom, has been divided
and scattered throughout the ages. Now,
a band of heroes, chosen for their extraordinary
gifts, find unexpected, passionate love while
braving dangers far beyond the present in a
desperate race against time....

Follow all four books in this thrilling new series
that concludes with *Time Raiders: The Protector*.

Time Raiders: The Seeker
(August 2009)
Lindsay McKenna

Time Raiders: The Slayer
(September 2009)
Cindy Dees

Time Raiders: The Avenger
(October 2009)
P.C. Cast

Time Raiders: The Protector
(November 2009)
Merline Lovelace

Books by Merline Lovelace

Silhouette Nocturne

Mind Games #37
*Time Raiders: The Protector #75

*Time Raiders

MERLINE LOVELACE

As an air force officer, Merline Lovelace served at bases all over the world, including tours in Taiwan, Vietnam and at the Pentagon. When she hung up her uniform for the last time, she decided to combine her love of adventure with a flair for storytelling, basing many of her tales on her experiences in the service.

Since then, she's produced more than seventy-five action-packed novels, many of which have made *USA TODAY* and Waldenbooks bestseller lists. Over ten million copies of her works are now in print in more than thirty-one countries.

When she's not glued to her keyboard, Merline and her husband enjoy traveling and chasing little white balls around the fairways of Oklahoma. Visit her Web site at www.merlinelovelace.com for information about other releases.

USA TODAY Bestselling Author

MERLINE LOVELACE

THE PROTECTOR

TIME RAIDERS

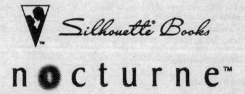

Silhouette Books

n🌑cturne™

SILHOUETTE BOOKS

ISBN-13: 978-0-373-61822-4

TIME RAIDERS: THE PROTECTOR

Recycling programs
for this product may
not exist in your area.

www.silhouettenocturne.com

Printed in U.S.A.

Dear Reader,

I absolutely loved participating in the TIME RAIDERS series with three of my favorite authors and sisters-in-arms—Lindsay McKenna, Cindy Dees and P.C. Cast. Not only are we all former military, we share a great love of history. We got to indulge that passion by hurling our characters back in time to search for pieces of a medallion that will have a staggering effect on the planet Earth.

When we were choosing the time periods for our books, I debated between two of my favorite historical eras—the early Viking period and the great cultural flowering of the Tang Dynasty in China. Then I thought, what the heck! Why not combine the two?

So sit back, relax and travel with two twenty-first-century Americans who, in the guise of intrepid adventurers from the land of icy fjords appear at the Imperial Court of the most powerful woman of the seventh century!

All my best,

Merline Lovelace

To the RomVets—
my sisters-in-arms and great writers one and all!
And most especially, the fabulous Lindsay McKenna,
Cindy Dees and P.C. Cast. Thanks for the wild ride
creating this wonderful series.

Preface

Fifty thousand years ago, after discovering that human females carry a nascent genetic potential that might one day develop into the ability to star navigate, the Pleiadian Council planted a dozen pieces of a bronze disk across the earth, hidden in darkness until mankind advanced enough to travel through time and find them.

And then, out of the ashes of the mystery-shrouded Roswell alien crash in 1947, arose a secret research project called Anasazi. Its improbable goal: learn to use the recovered alien technology for the purpose of time travel. General Beverly Ashton was the last to command this project before a dozen time travelers were inexplicably lost and the project disbanded.

However, the recent discovery of an ancient set of documents, the *Ad Astra* journals, has given Professor Athena Carswell the information she needs to begin sending modern time travelers back through human history in search of the twelve pieces of the Pleiadian Medallion, which, when fully reassembled, will send a signal to the council indicating mankind is ready to be introduced to the rest of the galactic community.

Project Anasazi has secretly been reactivated, and General Ashton, now retired, and Professor Carswell are continuing the project's work. They are carefully recruiting and training a team of military men and women to make the dangerous time jumps.

But threats loom on the horizon, both from

humans who would see the project ended, or worse, steal its work and use it for nefarious ends, and from the Centaurian Federation, which will do anything to stop humans from learning how to navigate the stars....

Chapter 1

Disorder is not sent down by heaven, it is produced by women.
—From the writings of Confucius

Frowning, USAF Major Max Brody wheeled his rental car through the nearly empty streets of Flagstaff, Arizona. The cold March dawn painted the snow-capped peaks surrounding the city in shimmering gold. Frost glittered on the buildings of Red Rock

University, dead ahead. His destination was a fenced-in compound set some distance apart from the main campus.

Max had been yanked out of his second tour of duty in Iraq and arrived here in Flagstaff only three days ago. He should have relished the snow and biting cold. Both went unnoticed, however, as he struggled to wrap his mind around the incredible mission he was about to undertake.

Starship navigators.

Pieces of a bronze medallion hidden in time.

Intergalactic power plays.

Earth's fate hanging in the balance.

The phrases ricocheted inside his head like shrapnel from an IED. If one of his troops had spouted those words, or any officer in his chain of command, Max would have pressed for an immediate psych eval.

But the mind-blowing phrases had come from retired USMC Brigadier General Beverly Ashton. She'd been Max's boss during a joint assignment years ago. He'd always considered her the best officer he'd ever served with. General Ashton had pulled every string in the book to get him released from his active duty unit for this special mission.

Only after Max had arrived in Flagstaff, bleary eyed from his long flight, did the general reveal she'd requested him because of his familiarity with the terrain targeted for a time jump.

Time jump. Jesus!

Max's gut twisted into a tight knot. After three days and nights of almost around-the-clock briefings, he still couldn't believe General Ashton's partner in this crazy enterprise, Professor Athena Carswell, had actually managed to harness the warps in time known as sine waves. Or that she did so using a crown-shaped headband retrieved from the crash of a UFO in New Mexico!

A world-renowned quantum physicist, Professor Carswell had worked with the military in her initial efforts to conqueror time and space. After repeated failures, however, the powers that be withdrew support for her Operation Anasazi.

But General Ashton had refused to give up. With the bulldog determination that was second nature to her, she'd kept the project alive with private funds and volunteers, most of whom were former military. And most of whom, Max had learned, possessed some form of psychic "gift" that made them open to the pulsing energy of the sine waves.

As unbelievable as it sounded, Professor Carswell's experiments had finally succeeded. Max had seen the proof. He'd also spoken to several mission specialists who'd traveled through time. Even more unbelievable, they'd returned with irregular-shaped sections of a medallion known variously as the Karanovo Stamp, the Pleiadian Disk and the Bronze Medallion. Each piece depicted various constellations. When all twelve sections were found and fitted together, the medallion could send a signal to an intergalactic council debating Earth's fate!

Given the enormous stakes, Max would have agreed to join their ranks even before he learned that his partner for the proposed "jump" was Cassandra Jones, a former air force weather officer—and the woman involved in the death of a friend of Max's from their Air Force Academy days.

Max's fists tightened on the steering wheel as he slowed for a turn. The board of inquiry had cleared Lieutenant Jones. Declared her innocent of all charges. So why had she abruptly resigned her commission and dropped out of sight?

Max intended to find out. His first priority on this mission was to locate the fourth piece of the medallion. That overrode all else. But his second and very private goal was to find out what really happened the day Captain Jerry Holland died.

His partner on this mission had no idea that Max even knew Jerry. He'd tell her when the time was right. And before this mission was over, Max would wring the truth from Cassandra Jones.

"Where is he?"

Quivering with nervous anticipation, Cassie slicked clammy palms down her thighs. She'd dressed casually for this mission in jeans and a maize-colored sweater, knowing she would soon jolt awake in another century wearing clothes appropriate to the time.

"Brody should have been here by now," she grumbled.

Unable to control her nervous energy, she paced the conference room some yards down the hall from the transport area.

"He'll be here shortly," General Ashton replied with her customary composure. Tall and blonde, with only a trace of silver at her temples, the retired USMC general still looked every inch the commander. "We don't launch for another hour," she added calmly.

As if Cassie needed the reminder!

She'd trained for this mission for months

while assisting with other jumps. Now it was her turn. And the mission was right up her alley.

She would jump back fourteen centuries and infiltrate the court of the most powerful woman of the seventh century. Empress Wu Jao, like all peoples of the ancient world, turned to shamans and sorcerers to predict weather conditions for ceremonies and major events. With one of the most significant events of Jao's reign fast approaching, Cassie would use her extraordinary sensitivity to atmospheric changes to gain the woman's confidence.

The remarkable ability to sense imminent weather changes was Cassie's gift…and her curse. Growing up in Oklahoma, she'd figured out at the tender age of three or four that when her naturally curly hair went limp and stretched in length there was a thunderstorm in the making. Or worse, a deadly tornado.

As she grew older she'd learned to interpret other natural occurrences. Like the faint ripples on the surface of a pond that indicated movement of the earth's underground plates. And birds going to roost low to the ground and fluffing their feathers to protect themselves from hail.

Cassie had tried, really tried, to channel her sensitivity to nature's nuances into productive uses. First by majoring in meteorology in college. Then by joining the air force as a weather officer. Unfortunately, the military was *extremely* skeptical of forecasts based on anything except data retrieved from high-tech instrumentation. So skeptical that Lieutenant Cassandra Jones had soon gained a reputation within the weather circles as a maverick.

That was the polite word for her intuitive predictions. Others had labeled them the product of a nutcase. Including the one man she'd thought she could love.

No! She wouldn't let herself think about Jerry Holland. Not now. Not with so much riding on this mission.

The arrival of her jump partner provided the impetus Cassie needed to shove aside the searing memories.

"'Bout time you got here, Major," she said, more brusquely than she'd intended.

Max Brody glanced at her from gray eyes as cool and hard as tempered steel. The rest of him wasn't much softer. Square jaw, square shoulders, square attitude. A combat engineer with more than twelve years of military experience, he sported buzz-cut blond hair and a don't-mess-with-me air.

He'd dressed down for the mission, too, but his jeans hugged muscled thighs and his faded Air Force Academy sweatshirt stretched across shoulders that would have done credit to an All-Pro guard. The man was six feet two inches of tough, uncompromising male.

"I'm ready if you are, Jones," he replied coolly.

"Excellent," General Ashton said briskly. "We'll do one final mission brief before you launch."

Cassie didn't need another brief. Every aspect of this mission was seared into her brain. It should be, after her weeks of prep.

Brody, on the other hand, had been a part of the Time Raiders team for all of three days. Knifing him with a look that said *pay attention*, she took a seat at the conference table. The major sat across from her.

With a flick of a switch, General Ashton illuminated the conference room's wall-size screen. Another flick brought up the digitized image of several leather journals with Latin inscriptions.

"These, as you know, are the *Ad Astra* journals Delia Sebastian brought back on one of her early jumps."

Ad Astra. To the stars. Appropriate, Cassie thought, for journals that had yielded the first clues to a major intergalactic power struggle.

Her heart bumped as the general glided a finger over a touch pad and aimed the on-screen pointer at a drawing in the middle of a page. There it was, the bronze medallion inscribed with various constellations.

Cassie's pulse kicked up another notch as General Ashton superimposed a digitized image over the original sketch. It showed three irregularly shaped pieces. Two of the pieces notched together. The third remained separate—waiting for the other pieces that would all fit together to form a smooth, round disk.

The general's blue eyes lingered on the three pieces for long moments before shifting to Cassie and Max. "If Professor Carswell has interpreted the message embedded in the third piece correctly, the fourth piece, the one you two will be looking for, was hidden in seventh-century China, at the court of the Tang emperors. I don't need to tell you how important it is that you find it."

"No, ma'am."

"Good. Professor Carswell's waiting for us in the transport area. If you don't have any questions about the target…"

"I'm good," Cassie said quickly.

Her jump partner gave a quick jerk of his chin. "Me, too."

Cassie's already humming nerves torqued even tighter as they left the conference room.

She'd assisted with other jumps. She'd helped debrief previous Time Raiders. She knew what to expect. Still, the sight of the capsule that would whisk her and Max Brody through fourteen centuries made her throat go dry.

The booth occupied center stage in the brightly lit area. A tall cylinder of glass, it contained two chairs, one for her, one for the major. That was it. No control console. No digital displays. No diodes to send electricity arcing through the air. The energy that would propel Cassie and Max through time would come from the brain of Professor Athena Carswell.

Gulping, Cassie dragged her gaze from the glass tube to the professor. A petite woman with soft brown curls and a heart-shaped face, she didn't look like your average genius of the Einstein variety.

Then again, Cassie didn't exactly fit the mold of your average seventh-century Chinese maiden. At five-seven, with intense green eyes, a fair complexion and hair that shaded more toward red than brown, she would stand out like a maypole at the Tang Dynasty court.

Which was why Professor Carswell had decided to send her back as an outlander— an emerald-eyed Irish sorceress captured by Vikings, sold into slavery and brought to the Imperial Court as a gift to the superstitious empress.

Cassie had to admit she wasn't too thrilled with that slave bit. Especially since uptight, stiff-spined Max Brody was going back as her "protector." His cover, too, had been carefully crafted. He was Bro-dai the Bold, a Viking warrior chosen by his chieftain to deliver Cassie to the court of the most powerful monarch on four continents.

She slanted him a quick glance, trying to decide what it was about Brody that rubbed her the wrong way. Maybe it was how he'd watched her during the past three days of mission prep, as if gauging her skills and readiness. Or how he seemed to weigh everything she said. She'd finally decided neither of those were bad traits in a partner whose life depended on his—and *her*—ability to survive in a time and a culture foreign to them both.

Brody had an edge over her in that regard. With degrees in both civil and mechanical engineering, he commanded one of the air force's premier combat construction squadrons. His hands-on expertise in Iraq repairing bomb damage had led the chief to put him in charge of coordinating United States military disaster relief efforts following China's devastating earthquake last year.

Brody had spent four months assisting with damage assessment and reconstruction in Sichuan Province. More important, he'd made several visits to Xi'an, once known as Chang'An. The city had served as China's capital for almost a thousand years before the seat of power was moved to Beijing. Brody's firsthand knowledge of the target area, General Ashton believed, would greatly facilitate this mission.

Cassie sure as hell hoped so! She stifled her doubts as Professor Carswell walked over to talk with them. Her brow creasing, the professor searched each of their faces in turn.

"You understand the process?"

They should. They'd been thoroughly briefed on the procedures to follow. Several times. Yet now that their jump was only moments away, both Cassie and Brody listened to her last mission brief intently.

"During the transport, I'll imbue each of you with the knowledge and language skills you'll need to survive in the seventh century. You'll arrive dressed in the appropriate clothing, at the site we've selected."

She reached into the pocket of her lab coat and withdrew two wide cuffs of beaten silver. An oval quartz crystal sat dead center in each bracelet.

"Once you put these bracelets on," the professor said, "*do not* take them off. The ESC is your escape, your only escape, if something goes wrong."

ESC. The acronym stood for emergency signal cuff, which pretty well said it all, in Cassie's opinion. She swallowed, slid the cuff over her wrist and pushed it up until it bit into the flesh of her upper arm. Max clamped his around his wrist.

"One last caution." The professor looked at each of them in turn, her expression grave. "From past jumps, I know I can smooth over any 'debris' you leave behind so there's no trace of your impact on history. But this only applies to actual historical events. If you're injured or killed, I can't make you whole, because you *were never really part* of that time period. So stay safe, and for God's sake, don't lose your ESC."

With that fervent plea, she ushered them into the transporter.

As they took their seats, Cassie could only admire Max's stoic calm. She knew he had to be a mass of raw nerves inside. He was the first—the only—person selected for a jump who didn't possess some kind of psychic skill. Professor Carswell was convinced it was that skill, that openness of mind and spirit, that made her volunteers so receptive to transport.

But time had become critical. The last three missions confirmed the fact that they weren't the only ones searching for the medallion pieces. Mysterious attacks on the lab and intruders breaking in to Professor Carswell's home pointed to the fact that someone here on earth wanted the power the medallion would give him or her.

Worse, they were also competing with hunters from another galaxy. Tessa Marconi had brought back living proof in the form of one very large, very powerful Centaurian who said that his former leader had vowed to keep humans from completing their search for the medallion.

So Max Brody and his intimate knowledge of China's ancient capital were Cassie's ticket to getting into the imperial palace, locating the fourth piece of the medallion and getting out again, fast!

Assuming she didn't lose him during the jump.

He wasn't one of their tight-knit Time Raiders cadre. Since he didn't possess a psychic power—none that had been documented, anyway—would he be lost, like the first travelers Carswell had sent back?

As the professor donned the weird crown with earpieces containing crystals matching the ones in their ESCs, Cassie reached out and gripped Max's hand. "We'll make it," she told him.

"We have to," he replied grimly.

His fingers threaded through hers and their eyes met. For that moment, that infinitesimal moment, they were bonded by excitement and fear.

"Hang on," he muttered.

It happened so fast, Cassie barely had time to register the tingle that raced across her skin and made the hair on her arms stand straight up.

One moment she was gasping as the temperature inside the capsule dropped a good forty degrees. In the next, an ugly, flat-nosed creature thrust its head through a swirling white haze and blasted her with the foulest breath in the history of the universe.

Chapter 2

A woman's duty is not to control or take charge.

—*Confucius*

"Get away from me!"

Shrieking, Cassie leaped back to escape the fearsome creature. She didn't move fast enough. It butted her shoulder and sent her flying into a mound of slushy snow. Hideous black gums and giant-size yellow teeth followed her down. Scuttling backward like an oversize crab, Cassie doubled her fist and swung with all her strength at the snapping jaws.

The creature brayed in pain and jerked its head up. And up. And up. Its long neck writhed like a furry python. Its hooves beat the earth in a frantic retreat.

A camel, Cassie realized when she'd blinked away the snowflakes clinging to her lashes. It was a camel! Complete with tasseled bridle and saddle.

A gloved hand shot out of the swirling white and grabbed the skittering animal's reins. Cassie followed the hand to an arm sleeved in rough wool. The sleeve led in turn to a wolf pelt draped over a set of broad shoulders, a bristling blond beard and a pair of eyes narrowed to slits under a flat-brimmed felt hat.

"Do you try to escape?"

"Huh?"

With a jerk of his chin, the stranger summoned an underling to take the camel's reins.

"Be warned, slave. Try again to escape, and I swear by Thor's hammer I will strip you naked and whip you to within an inch of your life."

Cassie's jaw dropped. That was Max under all those layers of beard and fur and wool. He'd made it! They both had!

Giddy with relief, she was still trying to assimilate that astounding fact when he grabbed her arm and hauled her to her feet.

"Hey! Back off, Brody."

His hand tightened brutally. A warning glinted in his steely eyes. "I am Bro-dai the Bold. Your master until I deliver you as I have been charged to do. You will address me with respect, slave, and speak in the tongues I have taught you."

Oooh-kay.

Cassie struggled to reset her mind to their new reality. She was astounded that Max had made the transition before her. Then again, he hadn't blinked awake to a gust of noxious camel exhaust.

She took a quick glance around to orient

herself. It was late afternoon, she noted, close to dusk. Misty gray clouds obscured a sun sinking fast toward snow-covered mountains. The faint glow of the rising moon shone through the haze above another mountain peak.

Squinting through the swirling snow, she saw she'd landed a short distance from a group of travelers. They were all bundled against the cold. Some wore coarse blankets across shoulders hunched under the weight of corded bundles or straw baskets. Others held on to the reins of pack animals or stood between the yokes of heavily ladened carts. All were watching the interaction between Cassie and Max with varying degrees of interest.

He played to the crowd by giving her arm a shake. "I will not tell you again, slave. You will address me with respect."

All right, already! She got the message and assumed a sullen scowl. "Yes, *master.*"

"We travel thousands of leagues to reach this point," he said in disgust, "and you fall from your saddle like a drunken Magyar."

That was one way of explaining their sudden drop into the seventh century, Cassie thought as she stamped her feet against the biting cold. A heavy cloak covered her from chin to knees. Beneath the cloak she wore a scratchy wool tunic, baggy pants and boots stuffed with straw. The pants, unfortunately, were soaked from her immersion in the icy slush. She twitched, trying to separate bare skin from clammy fabric, and glanced behind her. The massive castle looming out of the snow made her eyes widen.

Professor Carswell had delivered them right on target. They'd landed not twenty yards from the gates of the fortress guarding the mountain pass that led to China's ancient capital.

The fortress was part of the Great Wall, which snaked across steep peaks and ridges for almost four thousand miles. Damned if the fortifications didn't look every bit as formidable up close as they had in all the pictures Cassie had seen of them. She was

squinting through the snow at the high, undulating walls when Max gave her arm
another squeeze.

"Your duel with the camel drew the
guard's attention," he muttered under his
breath. "Keep your story straight."

Her heart thumped at the sight of the
heavyset figure tramping toward them. Bundled up in quilted cotton, leather armor, a
bronze breastplate and conical helmet, he
wore a distinctly unfriendly expression on
his face. The two soldiers trailing him hefted
vicious-looking pikes. *Not* the kind of men
Cassie had planned on messing with ninety
seconds into her mission.

"Move aside!"

The brusque command scattered the travelers waiting to pass through the gate. Merchants and wayfarers jumped out of the way.
Caravan tenders, dog-cart drivers and goat
herders shooed their animals aside.

Max stood his ground, his fingers still
digging in to Cassie's arm above her ESC.

"Who are you?" the guard demanded.

"And who is this female who screeches like a scalded cat?"

Amazing! She understood every word, every inflection. Professor Carswell was incredible.

"I am Lord Bro-dai," Max replied. "Vassal to a prince who rules a land where the sun does not set in summer. He has sent me to deliver this gift to your empress."

The guard didn't appear particularly impressed with the proposed gift. He raked Cassie with a contemptuous glance before addressing Max again. "Why would our most glorious empress want a lowly slave such as this one?"

"She is a seer, with powers that will astound all who witness them."

Sudden wariness replaced the guard's sneer. Like all people of his time, he feared the power of magicians and shamans as much as he revered it. His wariness increased as Max launched into their rehearsed spiel.

"My prince took the woman in a raid on an island with grass as green as her eyes. He

didn't know her powers until the witch con-
jured up a storm that almost sank our ship.
She's made this journey hell, too, by calling
down sandstorms, raging winds and now this
blizzard."

His eyes bulging, the sergeant of the guard
backed up a pace. Cassie half expected him
to cross his fingers in the age-old sign for
warding off evil spirits.

"Wait here," he ordered with nervous
bravado. "I must consult my captain."

Signaling to the two pikemen to keep
watch on them, he tramped back to the guard
post built into the wall beside the gates.
Cassie maintained her sullen expression as
she whispered an aside to Max. "He bought
it."

"So it seems."

"You want to ease up on the arm now?"

"Sorry." Max loosened his grip and let his
gaze drift toward the walls stretching into
the mists. "Unbelievable," he muttered
under his breath.

Well, thank God! She wasn't the only one

grappling with the fact they'd actually jumped fourteen centuries and landed smack in the middle of the Tang Dynasty. Despite his "me Viking, you slave" bluster, Max was still half in shock, too.

The wonder of it, the sheer incredibility, sizzled through Cassie's veins. She was here, mingling with travelers on the fabled Silk Road, waiting for permission to enter the empire historians agreed was the richest and most advanced of its era. An empire ruled for the first—and last!—time in its long history by a female.

If Athena Carswell was right, Empress Wu Jao possessed the fourth piece of the medallion, or knowledge of its location. She most likely didn't know the bronze piece's significance. Professor Carswell herself hadn't grasped that until she'd interpreted the *Ad Astra* journals. Now it was up to Cassie— and Max—to locate it.

Their quest hit an unexpected detour when the guard returned. He was accompanied by his captain and a mustached civilian draped in an exquisitely embroidered, fur-trimmed cloak. A dish-shaped fur hat covered most of his shaved head and topknot, leaving his long queue to swing from side to side as he strode forward and promptly took charge of the situation.

"I am Li Woo-An."

The captain of the guard stood back and said nothing. This was obviously Li's show. Cassie understood why with the man's next pronouncement.

"I am an inspector with the Bureau of Imperial Oversight and Protection of our Most Heavenly Majesties."

Oh, hell! No wonder the captain deferred to this civilian. The Bureau of Imperial Oversight, etc., etc., was the name given to the secret police force Empress Wu had created to spy on and eliminate her rivals. These guys made their twentieth-century counterparts in the Gestapo look like bumbling amateurs.

A whisper from a resentful slave, an anonymous note from a spurned lover, a twitch of a jealous concubine's eyebrows— any of those could result in princes and commoners alike being hauled in for "questioning" on trumped-up charges.

Once taken into custody, all suspects soon confessed to their crimes, whether real or imagined. No surprise there, since one of the bureau's favorite ways to extract confessions was to put the accused in an urn full of oil and light a fire under it. Entire families had been executed or forced to commit suicide based on such confessions. Cassie could almost feel the suspicion as Li addressed Max.

"You say this lowly slave is a seer?"

"She is."

The inspector's gaze cut to Cassie. His dark eyes burned into her for long moments. Then he looked around the crowd of gawking observers and hooked a finger at a porter bent almost double under the weight of the bundles strapped to his back.

"You! Come hence!"

"M-me, Excellency?"

"You."

Gulping, the man inched forward.

"On your knees."

The porter dropped, shaking from head to toe. A moan of terror escaped him as Li reached under his cloak and drew a dagger from a richly decorated sheath.

"Be still, you fool."

The man's terror turned to sobbing relief when Li sliced through one of the straps and tugged the topmost bundle free. With the cloth-wrapped package in one hand and the dagger in the other, Li turned to Cassie.

"Tell me what is bound up in this cloth, slave, or I will slit your throat and that of your master."

The crowd gave a collective gasp and shuffled closer, awaiting Cassie's answer with ghoulish eagerness. Max answered for her.

"She does not perform such foolish tricks," he said with a careless roll of his shoulders. "Her powers are not of that kind."

The crowd gasped again and Li's mouth

thinned beneath his drooping mustache. Cassie got the distinct impression the inspector wasn't used to being shrugged off.

"What kind *are* they?" he retorted dangerously.

"She foretells changes in nature. When rain will come, when trees will bud, when—"

"When this snow will cease to fall?" Li interrupted silkily.

"That, too, if the spirit is with her."

Li's gaze shifted to Cassie. "Speak, slave. Tell us when we will see the sun again."

Her heart thumping, she squinted at the hazy glow above the distant peak. The rising moon was brighter than when she'd spotted it a few moments ago. She was almost sure of it. And try as she might, Cassie couldn't detect a trace of red around it.

For a moment, just a moment, doubt squeezed her chest like a vise. Then she lifted her chin and went with her instincts. "The snow will cease this night and the sun will shine again come dawn."

The blunt response sent Max's stomach dropping straight to the tops of his sheepskin-lined boots. Jesus H. Christ! Couldn't she shade her answer a little more? Leave a wider margin of error?

Inspector Li obviously didn't care much for her boldness, either. "Your prophecy had best prove true, slave. If it doesn't, and snow still falls at dawn, you and your master will lose your heads."

Tossing the cloth bundle at the cringing porter, he shoved his dagger into its sheath and rapped out an order to the captain of the guard.

"Take them into the fort and hold them."

The guards relieved Max of his dagger and the sword strapped to his waist before escorting the prisoners through the gates and down a short flight of steps to a dank cell at the base of the wall. It contained no furnishings, no charcoal brasier for warmth, not even a slop bucket. The only light came from the barred grate in the door, and that was fading fast.

The moment the door clanged shut, Max rounded on his jump partner. "Are you out of your mind?"

She hugged her waist, trying to keep warm. "Not the last time I checked."

"Why didn't you give yourself more latitude with this snow business?"

"Back off, Brody. I know what I'm talking about."

Max hoped to hell she did. "How about cluing me in?" he retorted. "I'm not real anxious to abort our mission before it starts. Or get my head whacked off."

"Have you heard the old Zuni saying, 'If the moon's face is red, of water she speaks'?"

"You're risking our necks on an old saying?"

"You want it in more modern terminology? Okay." Shivering in the dank cold, she raised a hand and ticked off the points of her rationale. "A, a red halo around the moon or a shadow on its face is caused by cirrus clouds in the higher altitudes because B, these clouds contain ice crystals that refract the light. Ergo C—no red, no ice crystals, no snow."

"Does that hold true one hundred percent of the time?" Max asked suspiciously.

She chewed on her lower lip before admitting, "More like eighty to ninety."

"Dammit, Jones…"

"Look, you knew the risks when you agreed to the mission. Nothing about this operation is one hundred percent."

Nothing about this operation made a whole lot of sense, either, including the fact that he'd just zoomed through fourteen centuries.

"Didn't Confucius write something about the folly of putting women in charge?"

"Probably. The guy was a world-class misogynist. I bet you anything he was a Centaurian."

The reminder of the powerful forces arrayed against them snapped Max's brows together. He eyed his partner in this crazy enterprise and barked out a brusque order. "Take off your clothes."

"Excuse me?"

"You're soaked from the waist down and shivering like a lost dog. You need to get out of those wet clothes." Dragging the wolf pelt from his shoulders, he tossed it on the dirt floor. "You've been through military survivor training. You know the best way to keep warm is to share body heat."

"Yeah, right! Like I'm going to get naked and snuggle up with you."

"I'm not letting you catch pneumonia on my watch. Not with everything that's riding on this jump."

"Forget it, Brody."

"What's your problem?" Max snapped. "It's not like this would be the first time you got naked with a team member while deployed on a critical mission."

Well, hell! He hadn't meant to show his hand. Not yet. He'd wanted to get close enough to this woman to convince her to open up to him first.

The damage was done, though. He could see it in the way her face drained of all color and her green eyes went wide with shock.

"Wh…? What are you talking about?"

"I'm talking about you," he said, his jaw tight, "and Captain Jerry Holland."

She dragged her tongue over her lower lip. "How do you know about Captain Holland?"

"He was my roommate at the academy. We kept in touch over the years."

Max's eyes held hers, hard, unrelenting.

"I got an e-mail from him a couple days before he died. In it he mentioned a certain red-haired weather officer with killer legs and a tight, trim butt."

Max didn't intend it as a compliment. She didn't take it as one.

"Jerry said she was a tease who promised more than she delivered, but he was going to collect…if it was the last thing he ever did."

Chapter 3

Women and little people are difficult to handle.

—Confucius

He was going to collect...if it was the last thing he ever did.

The words stabbed into Cassie and left her bleeding inside. She'd thought she'd put it all behind her. The pain. The humiliation. The agonizing guilt.

She bled for another moment or two, then erupted into fury. It was either that or burst into tears, and she had no more left to cry.

"This is great! Just friggn' great! I'm soaked from the waist down. My lower half feels like an ice sculpture. I'm locked in a cell with the threat of beheading hanging over me and oh, by the way, the fate of the entire world on my back. And my partner in this enterprise wants to know if his buddy collected on his bet before he died."

She lunged forward and got toe-to-toe with Brody. If she'd learned nothing else from the disaster that had altered her life forever, it was to face her accusers head-on.

"Well, Jerry didn't collect. I delivered as promised, but he never made it back to camp to claim his winnings."

"Hold on a minute." Max's brows had snapped together. "Back up a little. What bet?"

"Oh, he didn't include that in his e-mail?" Her lip curled. "How he bet his pals that he'd get into the weirdo weather officer's pants? Find out if she was a freak in bed as well as out?"

She wouldn't let the pain and humiliation consume her again! She *wouldn't!*

Nor would she admit to Brody that she'd surrendered every part of herself to Jerry Holland on that lush tropical island. She'd bared her soul, told him about the taunts and jeers she'd endured as a child, recounted some of her problems with her military supervisors, only to hear him admit he considered her more than a little weird, too.

Writhing inside at the memory, she gritted her teeth and plowed on. "I tried to save him. That morning, just before the flash flood roared down on us, I tried to warn him."

But she'd left it too late.

It hadn't rained that much, only a few inches upriver. Yet she'd spotted leaves and debris carried on the rushing current and heard—or thought she'd heard—a distant roar. If she hadn't caught Jerry bragging to another squad member that he'd won the

Lieutenant Jones bet... If he hadn't tried to brazen it out when she'd confronted him... If she hadn't been so hurt and mortified and seething with white-hot fury...

"Our mission that day was classified," Cassie finished, wiping every trace of emotion from her voice. "I can't tell you where we were or what we were doing, but I can tell you this. During the official inquiry into Captain Holland's death, two other squad members testified that I urged him to move our location to higher ground." Her eyes locked with Brody's. "And that's all I intend to tell you."

No way was she going to admit the paralyzing doubts Jerry's tragic drowning had embedded in her psyche. How she'd questioned her skills, her judgment, her very femininity for long afterward.

She'd confided those doubts to Professor Carswell and General Ashton when she'd volunteered for Operation Anasazi. She'd also told them as much as she could of her last, disastrous mission. She owed them that honesty.

Athena Carswell had looked deep into her eyes and read the truth. General Ashton had gone with her gut. As a result, Cassie would trust either of those women with her life. But hell would do the proverbial big freeze before she trusted another man with her heart.

Especially one who suspected she knew more than she had admitted concerning the death of his buddy!

"Your turn," she grunted. "Why did you—?"

Cassie broke off, shuddering violently. When she continued, her teeth clicked like castanets.

"Why did you agree to…jump back in time with…someone you obviously…don't trust?"

"General Ashton vouched for you. Said you were the only one with the skill to make this jump." Frowning, he raked a hand through the shaggy, sun-streaked blond hair that matched his beard. "I trust the general's judgment. Implicitly. Then there's that small matter you mentioned about the fate of the entire world hanging on this mission."

"But…?"

"But that e-mail raised questions in my mind. I wanted answers."

"Are you…satisfied with them?"

Not hardly, Max thought. But if he didn't do something soon, his jump partner would turn blue right before his eyes.

"For now. Let's get you warm."

"No…thanks. I'd rather snuggle up…with that garbage-breathing camel."

"You can snuggle with him tomorrow. Tonight you're stuck with me."

She was shivering too violently to protest further. Or to send the signal that they'd arrived at their prescribed destination. After two fumbling attempts to bury a hand under her heavy cloak and reach the cuff banding her upper arm, she gave up.

Max shook his head. "I'll do it."

Rolling back his sleeve, he clapped his hand over the quartz crystal in his own silver cuff. When the quartz warmed under his palm, he gave it two quick taps.

"Signal sent. Now take off your clothes."

"They made it! Both of them!"

Athena Carswell's exultant shout cut like a saber through the tension in the lab. Beverly Ashton and the two mission specialists who'd joined them for the nerve-racking vigil following the jump exploded into whoops.

"Yes!"

Her brown-gold eyes blazing with relief, Delia Sebastian threw herself into Jake Tyler's arms. She'd made more jumps than any other Time Raider. She knew how dangerous every attempt to cross time and space could be.

Bev had to smile at the wet, sloppy kisses Delia planted all over Jake's face. These two were her protégés. She'd handpicked them, as she had every other Operation Anasazi volunteer. That Delia and Jake had managed to survive *and* rekindle the love they'd once had for each other caused a little ache just under her ribs.

Bev had had a love like that once. So long ago that she had to work hard to recall the face of the cocky marine chopper pilot she'd married as a young lieutenant, then lost in a fiery crash.

Bev had buried her grief by throwing herself into Project Anasazi. Over time, the pain had dulled. It was only at moments like this, as she watched Delia and Jake's unrestrained joy, that she ached for someone to share hers with, too.

"All right, you two," she said with a smile. "Deep-six those public displays of affection. Which one of you has the watch tonight?"

They broke apart, wearing identical sheepish grins.

"I do," Jake responded.

The lab was manned 24/7 during a jump, and Athena occupied the sleeping quarters set up nearby. If either Cassie or Max sent an emergency signal, the entire crew would work to bring them back, and fast.

"I'll back Jake up," Delia asserted. "Go home, ma'am. Get some sleep. We'll notify you if we receive any further contact."

Bev didn't argue. She felt every hour of the three intense days of mission prep, and every minute of the nerve-racking wait for the team to verify they'd made the jump. She could use a hot shower, a glass of chilled Riesling and a couple of pine logs blazing away in the kiva fireplace of her Flagstaff condo.

"You'd better get some sleep, too, Athena," Bev murmured, noting the slump to the physicist's shoulders under her lab coat. "These jumps take so much out of you."

"Yes, they do." Triumph threaded through the weariness in the professor's voice. "But we got them there, Bev. Cassie and Max. They'll find the fourth piece of the medallion. I know they will."

She left unsaid the unimaginable consequences if they didn't. No one in the lab needed the reminder.

Certainly not Bev, as she tugged up her

coat collar to block the knifing wind while she walked to her car. Like Athena, she'd lived, breathed, slept and eaten Project Anasazi for almost ten years. She knew what hung in the balance.

She'd also used every trick in the book to fend off the determined efforts of the shadowy figure determined to claim the medallion and the power it would give him. Bev still didn't have his name. Not yet. But she was close.

One of the private investigators she'd hired after break-ins at the lab and at Athena's home had disappeared. The second had phoned a few days ago to say he was following a money trail with more switchbacks than a python with a severe case of indigestion. He promised to stay with it, though, and discover who the hell was funding these illegal activities.

Then, of course, there were the Centaurians. Powerful alpha males from a distant galaxy who'd mastered the ability to navigate the stars. Unwilling to share their power, the Centaurians systematically suppressed that ability in others—including earth females who possessed the nascent star navigator gene. From previous jumps, Bev and the others knew the ruthless leader of the Centaurians had sent his men in under the radar of the Pleiadean Council to conduct search-and-destroy missions on earth.

They'd done a helluva a job of it. Earth's early matriarchal societies had all but disappeared over the millennia as men assumed more and more dominant roles. Organized religions had contributed to that process by decreeing only men could be priests and prophets. Even today, with women performing absolutely essential roles in the military, there were still throwbacks who felt females didn't belong in uniform.

Bev's jaw tightened as she steered through the snowy streets to her condo. Every team she and Athena had sent to search for pieces of the medallion had done battle with a Centaurian. Tessa Marconi had not only clashed with one, she'd conquered his heart and brought him back with her.

What Lord Rustam had related about his people had struck chills into his listeners' hearts. Although Centaurians could assume any shape, any form, they retained vestiges of the half horse, half human centaurs that had originated their race. Some had toes that were joined, almost like a hoof. Others sported the remnants of a mane, as evidenced by the ruff of coarse hair that ran halfway down their backs.

Only the strongest were allowed to mate, however. The rest were gelded and used for menial tasks. And only one claimed the absolute right to mount any female he chose.

Kentar of the Fifth Nebula.

The very name raised Bev's hackles. After what the bastard had put her mission specialists through, she wished fervently he would show his face. Just once. She knew how to wield a knife. Ole Kentar would whinny on back to his galaxy a gelding.

That fierce vow was uppermost in her mind when she pulled onto the interstate. Two miles later, she spotted a vehicle parked on the shoulder, its hazard lights blinking. A little farther on she spied the driver trudging along with his shoulders hunched against the snow. As Bev approached, he turned and squinted at her.

"Oh, hell!"

The rimless glasses and pink plaid Burberry scarf wrapped around his throat identified the man immediately. Prissy, officious Allen Parker chaired the architectural committee of Bev's condo association. At the best of times, he was barely tolerable. At the worst, he was a royal pain in the ass.

She was tempted to zing on down the highway. Very tempted. She was in no mood for Parker right now. Unfortunately, her conscience wouldn't let her pass a stranded motorist, even one as obnoxious as Parker. Sighing, Bev pulled over and opened her Bronco's door to shout, "Need a ride?"

"Yes!"

When he minced toward her through the slush, Bev rolled her eyes. Thank God for

strong males like Jake Tyler, and Alex
Patton's fierce Celtic warrior, Cardoc. Even
Tessa's Centaurian, Lord Rustam. They'd
provided the kind of muscle and brain power
on previous jumps that had complimented
their partners' skills and strengths.

As would Max Brody. Bev didn't doubt
that for a minute. She'd seen him in action,
knew what he was capable of. Knew, too, he
would more than match Cassie's fierce determination to find the next piece in this
damnable puzzle.

She drummed her fingers on the steering
wheel, waiting for Parker, wondering how her
missions specialists were doing in their quest.

Cassie lay on her side, her back to Max's
front, his left arm hooked over her waist.
The wolf pelt under them provided mini-
mal cushioning against the dirt floor. His
cloak was draped over them both. She
might have rejoiced in the heat transfer-
ring from his body to hers if her every
thought, every effort, hadn't been concen-

trated on keeping her butt from making contact with his groin.

They'd been snuggled together off and on for almost three hours. Cassie had been a twisted bundle of nerves the whole time. She still wore several layers up top. A linen blouse of sorts, a woolen shirt and her cloak. Below that, however, she was bare—and all too conscious of the bulge that poked her bottom every time she shifted.

Like now. One twitch, and she bucked like a bee-stung mare.

"What's the matter?" Max drawled in her ear. "Can't find a comfortable position?"

She was damned if she'd admit her ridiculous nervousness was the result of the feel of his hard, muscled body curved around hers.

"In case you haven't noticed, Brody, it's still snowing."

"Yeah," he muttered, less sarcastic now. "I've noticed."

The barred grate in their cell door was only a few inches square, barely big enough to let in a few errant flakes.

"The window faces west," Cassie said grimly. "The moon rises in the northeast quadrant tonight. If it shines through the clouds, we won't be able to see it. Which means we won't know if it shows red."

His arm tightened on her waist, drawing her closer. A reflex action, she thought. Hoped!

"We'd better try and get some sleep," he muttered. "We may need to fight our way out of here come dawn."

Sure… She would just close her eyes and nod right off. No sense worrying about their mission. No reason for her nerves to jump every time his breath tickled the fine hair at the back of her neck.

Think of the Ad Astra *journals,* she told herself sternly. *Think of the Pleiadian Council. Think of the Centaurians, so determined to crush all those with star navigator potential. Think of—*

"Christ! You're stiff as a board, Jones. Relax. Nothing's going to happen until dawn."

With a little grunt, he shifted and raised his

right knee. Hers came up with it, and the rough hair of his leg brushed her sensitive inner thigh.

Was he doing it on purpose? Trying to throw her off balance with these moves, as he had when he'd tossed Jerry's name at her? If so, the ploy was working. She couldn't think about anything but the feel of him pressed against her from neck to knees.

Squeezing her eyes shut, Cassie forced herself to relax. She wouldn't be any good to herself or to her jump partner come morning if she didn't get at least a few hours' sleep.

Despite his loose sprawl, Max kept every sense on full alert. So alert he picked up on the change in Cassie's breathing while she was still drifting through that half state before sleep.

Even then she didn't completely relax. Her body remained stiff and unyielding until she gave a last, jerky twitch and sank into oblivion.

Max wished to hell he could follow her

lead. Almost as much as he wished he could believe his flat assertion that nothing would happen until dawn.

He'd thrown that out for her benefit. He'd had to do something to counter his monumental stupidity in bringing up his knowledge of her past. He'd intended to get her to trust him, make her *want* to tell him what had really happened the day Jerry died. Instead he'd heaped more tension on a woman already coiled tight.

Not real smart, when he had to depend on her skills to gain entrée to the empress's inner circle and find the medallion piece. Max would have to work hard to regain his jump partner's confidence.

He settled her head more comfortably on his arm as he picked up the thump of tramping boots and the dull clank of steel that had to signal a changing of the guard. The sound of subdued voices carried on the cold air. Something that might be ivory dice clattered across a board.

Scents drifted through the barred grate.

Smoldering charcoal. Sizzling meat. Max's stomach rumbled in response. Yet the hunger that snaked through his belly had nothing to do with the fact that he hadn't eaten since breakfast. To his profound disgust, his body was reacting to the one nested against it. The feel of her, the scent of her, stirred a response he had *not* expected.

Grimacing, Max eased his knee from between hers and put a little space between their lower bodies.

Cassie blinked awake before dawn. The cell was still filled with inky blackness. She had no idea what time it was, but she didn't want to be caught with her pants down, literally *or* figuratively.

"Max."

She got an inarticulate grunt in response, and poked at the solid wall of chest pinning her to the wolf pelt.

"Roll over."

Another grunt. Cassie poked harder.

"You're squashing me. Roll over."

She scrambled out from under him and dragged his cloak with her. Draping it around her hips, she groped for her clothing.

The baggy pants were still clammy, but Cassie gritted her teeth and pulled them on before shoving her feet into her straw-filled boots. Good thing, as a heavy tread sounded outside the cell just moments later.

A key rattled in the lock. The door was flung open. Flickering torches sent up smoky trails as Inspector Li ducked under the low lintel.

Cassie's heart pounded. She couldn't see outside through the smoke of the torches. Had modern science and ancient Zuni wisdom held true, or was it still snowing?

She sensed Max coming to stand behind her. The soldiers had confiscated his sword and dagger, but he and Cassie both still had their silver cuffs. If it *was* still snowing, they might well have to abort the mission almost before it got started.

She edged her right hand across her body, slid it under the opposite sleeve. Her fingers inched upward, toward the cuff.

Max moved closer. She could feel him behind her, feel the tension radiating from his body until Inspector Li ended the suspense with a terse announcement.

"The snow ceased to fall an hour ago."

He sounded almost disappointed, although his mood was hard to read with that drooping mustache and face that looked as if it hadn't cracked a smile in the past century.

"You will leave for Chang'an within the hour. The guards will take you to the latrines to relieve yourselves and wash, and to the mess for breakfast. Then I myself will escort you to the imperial palace."

Chapter 4

*A woman ruler is as unnatural as a hen
crowing like a rooster at daybreak.*
                                    —Confucius

The cavalcade left the Great Wall fortress in
the thin gray light of dawn.

Inspector Li rode at the head of the troop.
He was mounted on a well-muscled chestnut
with the sloping shoulders, strong joints
and hard hooves of the Sanhe breed. The

troops accompanying them were similarly mounted. *Sanhe,* Cassie knew from her intense mission prebrief, translated to "three rivers." Appropriate, considering the sturdy horses were bred on the vast, grassy plain fed by the three rivers that also served as vital shipping arteries for China's ancient capital.

Max and Cassie were given similar mounts so their plodding camel wouldn't slow the troop down. Thank God! Cassie was more than happy to have seen the last of Garbage Breath. She scrambled into the saddle of a Sanhe and took her place in the small cavalcade.

Heavily armed soldiers rode in front and behind them. The troops were dressed uniformly in helmets, leather breastplates threaded with small steel disks and baggy trousers. The steel sections clinked in rhythm with the jingle of their bridles and stirrups.

Inspector Li was apparently so sure of his troop's muscle that he'd ordered the guards to return Max's sword and dagger. Max strapped on the sword and shoved the dagger into its scabbard. Then—at last!—they were on their way to China's ancient capital.

The first part of the journey was almost straight down as they descended from the high mountain pass. Thick forests of pine and fragrant cypress shrouded the road on either side. Accumulated snow adorned the tree branches, as well as the roofs of the way stations they passed, but by midmorning the sun had taken some of the cold sting from the air.

A final winding turn gave Cassie and Max their first glimpse of the broad plain at the base of the mountains. Wheat and soybean fields lying fallow in the winter sun stretched in an endless patchwork quilt. Interspersed among the fields were small farms, each with its own grove of mulberry trees. The branches were bare now but come spring their thin, glossy leaves would feed the worms that produced the gossamer thread woven into silk by the farmers' wives.

As the troop clattered along the road

cutting straight as an arrow across the plain, the sun blazed bright in the winter sky. Cassie began to sweat under her cloak, woolen shirt and linen shift. Her stockinged feet swam inside the straw-filled boots. She itched to shed some of her layers, but had to wait until they made a short stop at noon to peel off her cloak and pluck out the insulating straw.

Max removed his cloak, too, but kept the wolf pelt. The fur rode across his shoulders like a shaggy mantle. Cassie had to admit the thing made for a dramatic effect. So did Max. With his bristling blond beard and the long hair he'd tied back with a leather thong, he looked every inch the Viking warrior he was supposed to be.

Li barely gave his men time to water the horses and gobble down a handful of boiled rice before issuing a terse order to remount. Cassie reached for her mount's iron stirrup and started to climb into the saddle, but shrieking thigh muscles stopped her midlift.

"Yikes!"

Max whipped his head around. "What?"

"I'm, uh, a little stiff."

She gripped the pommel with both hands and managed to swing into the hard wooden saddle. She could tell from Max's sardonic expression it wasn't a graceful move. Ignoring him, she shoved her other foot into the stirrup.

"Next stop," she announced with grim satisfaction, "the Imperial City!"

Chang'an rose out of the vast rolling plain like the fabled city of every ancient tale Cassie had ever read or heard. Its massive walls were visible from miles away, as were the multitiered roofs of its many temples and bell towers.

She wasn't surprised by its size or obvious splendor. Chang'an served as the capital of a enormously wealthy empire that stretched from the Pacific almost to India, and from Korea in the north to Vietnam and Burma in the south. Incredibly, the city supported a population of more than a million.

At least half of the inhabitants seemed to be on the road, either going into or coming out of the walled city. The closer Inspector Li's cavalcade got, the denser the traffic. Finally an impatient Li ordered two soldiers to dismount and march ahead, banging on cymbals to clear a path.

"Make way! Make way for Inspector Li!"

The dreaded title of "inspector" had more effect than the cymbals. Peddlers pushing handcarts, farmers driving wagons ladened with produce, even red-robed Buddhist monks threw fearful looks over their shoulders and edged aside.

As the troop approached the walled city, Cassie spied tall mounds dotting the landscape to the north. Burial mounds, she realized with a gulp. Chinese emperors from as far back as the second century BC had built elaborate tombs in this fertile region—including the first Qin emperor, who'd had an army of larger-than-life-size terra-cotta warriors constructed to guard him in the afterlife.

They were out there somewhere, those

thousands upon thousands of clay figures, already buried in the mists of time and more than eight hundred years of changing dynasties. Amazing to think they would remain just a legend until 1974, when a farmer sinking a rod for a well would stumble on one of the greatest archaeological treasures of all time.

"Make way for Inspector Li!"

Preceded by the clash and clang of cymbals, the troop entered Chang'an through a massive gate topped by a guard tower painted bright red.

The city was laid out in a grid. Its wide, tree-lined streets were aligned at angles as prescribed by the soothsayers to form precise city blocks. Each block formed a lively neighborhood, a *hu tong,* that boasted its own temples and bazaars and schools for young boys.

On this bright winter day, people filled the broad streets. Cassie marveled at their rich cultural diversity as she surveyed wealthy Chinese in fur-trimmed silk robes rubbing elbows with scholars in blue cotton tunics that reached to their slippered feet. There were foreigners, too, traders and explorers and envoys from distant lands who had followed the fabled Silk Road to its terminus here at Chang'an. Cassie spotted white-robed Muslims and black-bearded Hasidic Jews mingling with turbaned Indians and fierce-looking Mongols.

Noise hammered at her from all sides as they rode toward the walls separating the Imperial City from the rest of Chang'an. Temple bells chimed. Deep-throated gongs boomed the hour. Merchants hawked their wares from open shop fronts, while monks chanted their prayers, acrobats clacked wooden balls in the air and what sounded like hundreds of birds whistled and tweeted from wicker cages in the bird market.

The smells were just as intense. Incense from local temples, dumplings frying in vats of sizzling oil, steaming dung waiting for the street sweepers to collect it—all combined for a nose-twitching experience. Then their party passed through another massive gate, and the sheer size of the imperial palace drove everything else from Cassie's mind.

"Wow," she murmured, awestruck.

The palace complex constituted a city within a city, with an outer section lesser mortals could enter and an inner one restricted to the royal family and their servants. The cobbled outer court had to be at least two football fields in length. It was ringed by barracks for the imperial guards, temples, audience halls and the houses of wealthy nobles and high-ranking officials. Cassie was gawking openly at the richly adorned roofs and elaborate facades of some of these houses when Li halted his mount and swung out of the saddle.

"At last," she muttered as she and Max dismounted, as well. "I'm aching in muscles I never knew I had."

He sent her a quick frown, as if assessing whether her aches and pains could affect their mission. "I'll see if I can scrounge some horse liniment later and rub you down."

"Sure. Just what I need to make a splash at the sophisticated Chinese court. Clothes reeking of camel and skin that smells of eau d'horse liniment."

His frown relaxed into a half grin. "Yeah, you are pretty aromatic."

Damn! What a difference when he dropped his tough-man persona and grinned like that. It did things to her insides. Hot, tingling things.

To cover her absurd reaction, Cassie gave a snort. "Have you had a whiff of yourself lately, wolf man?"

The banter helped ease some of her tension, but adrenaline rushed back with a vengeance when Inspector Li strode over to them.

"You will wait here," he informed Max. "I'll send word to the empress of this gift you have brought her. If she deigns to accept it, I will accompany you into the reception rooms."

And take full credit for escorting the gift to the imperial palace, Cassie guessed shrewdly.

She used the wait to visit one of the courtyard's ornate fountains. Before facing the
most powerful woman in the world, she
needed to wash away the grime of their
journey and a night spent on a dirt floor. Half-
naked. With her bare butt nested on Max's
thighs.

The memory of those dark, intimate hours
bumped Cassie's pulse up several notches.
She stole a look at the man next to her,
splashing water over his face and hands. To
her profound disgust, her bird's-eye view of
his wide shoulders and rippling muscles
worked a number on her insides again.

Dammit! She had to stop doing this!
Brody was Jerry's friend. He'd made it clear
last night he didn't completely trust her.
More to the point, he was her partner on this
jump. No way she was repeating past mistakes by getting physical with him.

Still, she couldn't help edging closer to
Max when Li and another man emerged from
a pillared doorway almost an hour later. The
inspector crooked an imperious finger at them.

"Come! Our Most Heavenly Majesty, Empress Wu, has agreed to see you. Chief Eunuch Tai will escort us into her presence."

"Showtime," Max murmured under his breath. "You ready?"

"As I'll ever be," Cassie gulped.

The man with Li towered over him by five or six inches. His head was shaved except for his topknot, which was held in place with gold pins. His exquisitely embroidered silk robe sheathed an impressive set of shoulders and bulging biceps. He must have developed those before he was castrated and ran out of testosterone, Cassie guessed.

Unusual, since she'd read that most eunuchs at the Chinese court were castrated as young boys by parents hoping to secure a lucrative position for their son. As palace insiders, eunuchs could acquire power and wealth that often rivaled princes. She'd also read that half of the boys who went under the knife died from shock or blood loss or infection.

Castration of young males wasn't unique

to China, of course. Nor was it confined to the ancient world. European opera buffs had thrilled to the soprano or mezzo-soprano notes of castrati well into the nineteenth century. Boys in the Vatican choir were emasculated right up until the 1870s to preserve their angelic voices.

But the primary historical impetus behind the practice of employing eunuchs inside harems and palaces was to keep women chaste and subservient to one man. A sultan or king could have a hundred or more wives or concubines, but they serviced only him. By ensuring his women were watched and tended by eunuchs, the king could also ensure any children they produced sprang from his seed alone.

This particular eunuch looked Cassie over with eyes both assessing and shrewd before bowing politely to Max.

"I am Tai Kin Su, Chief Eunuch of the Lotus Court of the Imperial Palace. Please come with me."

He led them through a succession of corridors and audience chambers, each more sumptuous than the last. The predominant color was red. Pillars, tapestries, furnishings all glowed with that vibrant color, although the royal yellow grew more visible as they entered the main reception area.

Finally they approached a massive pair of red doors studded with brass knobs set in rows of nine. At a nod from Tai, two guards grasped the doors' brass rings.

"On your knees," the eunuch instructed calmly. "Keep your forehead to the floor as you crawl forward. Do not raise your face to the empress until she desires you to."

Inspector Li had already dropped to his knees. Cassie glanced at Max and saw he didn't like the idea of kowtowing and crawling in any more than she did. Lifting her chin, she addressed Tai. "This is not my way."

Inspector Li whipped his head around. "Silence, slave! You will do as ordered."

Cassie ignored him. Folding her arms across her chest, she locked eyes with Tai.

The inspector might have balls, but the eunuch had the power in this situation.

"I am a princess in my own land and a respected shaman. You may drag me into the empress's presence by my hair, but I will not crawl. Such is not my way."

Infuriated, Li leaped to his feet and lashed out with a bunched fist. Max blocked the blow with an upflung arm.

"This woman is in my keeping until the empress deigns to accept her," he told Li, steel in every word. "Until that time, no man but me touches her."

His face suffused with fury, Li turned to the eunuch for a decision.

Tai's gaze was locked on the silver cuff banding Max's wrist. When Max dropped his arm, the eunuch's shrewd eyes shifted to Cassie and swept from her tangle of dark red hair to her snow-stained boots.

"A wise man," he said finally, "adapts himself to circumstances, as water shapes itself to the vessel that contains it."

Huh? Cassie was still trying to figure out

who was supposed to shape to what when the eunuch signaled the guards.

"We proceed."

The massive red doors groaned open. Tai murmured to the ornately uniformed official just inside. The official rapped his staff on the floor three times and announced their presence in a booming voice.

"Inspector Li of the Bureau of Imperial Oversight, Chief Eunuch Tai of the Lotus Court and Lord Bro-dai from the Land of the Night Sun, with the gift of a slave/seer for Your Most Heavenly Majesty."

Li and Tai entered the hall on hands and knees, foreheads bumping the floor. When Max and Cassie walked in behind them, gasps rose from the scholars and officials already in the hall. More than one imperial guard reached for his sword. Then all eyes turned to the slender woman seated on a gold throne at the far end of the hall.

Cassie's first impression was that Wu Jao looked closer to thirty than the fifty Cassie knew her to be. Small and delicate, the empress exuded an aura of almost fragile beauty.

It just showed how deceptive appearances could be. Those rosebud lips and doelike eyes masked a brilliant mind and a will of tempered steel, Cassie knew.

The daughter of a high-ranking princess, Wu Jao had been taught to play the flute, sing, write and read the classics. At thirteen, she'd joined the court of the first Tang emperor as a fifth-level concubine. Her wit and charm had enchanted him *and* his son so much that when the father died, the son brought her back to court as his second-level concubine.

In the years that followed, Wu bore Junior several sons, and oh, by the way, convinced him to execute his first empress and give her the title. Skilled at the game of power politics, she took the reins of government into her own hands following her husband's stroke. He was still alive, but a mere figurehead, rarely brought out anymore even for ceremonial occasions.

At age fifty, the woman was just reaching her prime, Cassie knew. After her husband's death, Wu would put her third son on the throne, then depose him; then put her fourth son in power and depose him. Finally, she would declare herself sole and supreme ruler. When she died at the age of eighty-two, she would have ruled the vast Chinese empire with an iron fist for more than half a century.

Assuming, of course, that Cassie and Max didn't screw with history. Or lose their heads while attempting to screw with history. That possibility appeared more likely with each step they took.

The empress watched them, her eyes unblinking beneath her elaborate headdress. It had to be at least a foot high, a complicated arrangement of braids and loops of glossy black hair adorned with gold and pearl ornaments. More pearls were draped around her neck. Ropes and ropes of them. So thick and lustrous they almost obscured the curvaceous breasts enticingly displayed by her low-cut silk gown.

But nothing could obscure the lethal note

in her voice when she addressed Max. "Do you offer me gift, Lord Bro-dai from the Land of Night Sun, or insult?"

"Gift, most gracious and beautiful queen. I bring you a seer with great powers."

Wu's gaze shifted to Cassie. She clicked her gold-and-jewel-sheathed nails on the arm of the throne, then turned her attention back to Max.

"What kind of powers?"

"She foretells changes in weather."

"He speaks the truth, Majesty." From his prone position, Li dared to interject an endorsement. "I tested her myself."

"Did you?"

When the empress turned a thoughtful glance her way, Cassie's heart thumped against her sternum so loudly she was sure the entire court could hear.

Professor Carswell had picked this year, this month and this day for their jump for a specific reason. One of the major events in Wu's long reign was fast approaching. At this point, she still governed in her husband's name. Less than two weeks from now, she would declare herself co-regent and drop the pretense that he had any say in matters. *If,* that is, the omens were favorable and the gods sent good weather for the magnificent ceremony that would celebrate her grab at power.

Cassie didn't move, didn't so much as breathe, while Wu Jao looked her over.

"If she is a seer, why does she wear the rags of a slave?"

"She *is* a slave," Max answered. "We captured her during a raid."

"And she cannot use her powers to escape you?"

"Not while I wear this." He raised his arm to display the silver cuff around his wrist. "I took it from the high priest of her clan. She wears a similar band."

"Show me."

Cassie went into her sullen slave routine as Max yanked up her arm. The sleeves of her woolen shirt and linen shift fell back. He pushed them up farther and tapped the quartz oval in the center of her armband.

"This crystal channels her powers to the crystal in my cuff. For better or worse, we are bound together until she passes into the possession of another strong enough to harness her powers."

"Such as I," the empress said, not doubting herself for a moment.

"Such as you," Max echoed.

Wu Jao's gaze lingered on his face for several moments. "Before I decide whether to accept such a gift, I would hear more of her powers, and of the land from whence she comes. Tai!"

The eunuch raised his head. "Yes, Most Heavenly Majesty?"

"Find quarters for Lord Bro-dai and the slave." The empress's nose wrinkled delicately. "While I speak with him further, you will see that she is bathed. She stinks of camel and horse dung. Once she is fit for my presence, I will require a demonstration of her skills."

"Yes, Majesty."

With a last, telling look at Max, Cassie allowed herself to be led away.

"Interesting that Lord Bro-dai's stink didn't offend the empress's sensibilities," she muttered to the eunuch when they'd exited the audience hall and started down a long corridor.

"On some men, the smell of sweat and horse offends our most gracious empress. On others, it does not." He slanted her an enigmatic glance. "She has varied and, some would say, strong appetites."

Uh-oh! Cassie could guess which appetites he referred to. Tai's next comment confirmed her suspicions.

"With the emperor no longer able to take her to his bed, it's rumored she looks elsewhere for her pleasure."

"Rumored?"

"Rumored," he repeated flatly. "There is no way to substantiate the tales. There will never be. No man who enjoyed the empress's favor would live long enough to speak of it to others."

Double uh-oh!

Cassie had spent several sleepless hours

last night trying not to bump up against Max. If asked, she could personally verify he came very well equipped.

Then there was that wicked grin. And that damned wolf pelt. The man practically shouted hot, sweaty, down-and-dirty sex. The kind any woman, empress or otherwise, would drop her silk drawers for.

Cassie just hoped to hell Bro-dai the Barbarian could keep his pants buttoned long enough to help her find the medallion!

Chapter 5

Those who cannot be taught, cannot be
instructed. These are women and eunuchs.
                                    —Confucius

When the cell phone clipped to her waist
broke into the Marine Corps anthem, Bev
glanced down. The sight of her neighbor's
name flashing up on caller ID made her
grimace.

She'd been at the lab since early morning,

hoping against hope either Max or Cassie would signal that they'd recovered the fourth piece of the medallion and were requesting an immediate return.

It was far too early for those hopes. Bev knew that. Yet she'd hung around the lab anyway, and passed the hours by reviewing folders on potential future jumpers. The last thing she was in the mood for right now was a conversation with her prissy neighbor.

Her cell phone belted out another stanza of "From the Halls of Montezuma." Sighing, she unclipped the instrument and flipped up the lid.

"Hi, Parker. Did you get your car fixed?"

"I did. And I'd like to thank you for coming to my rescue yesterday by inviting you to dinner tonight."

"That's not necessary. Neighbors are supposed to help each other out."

"I insist. Shall we say seven o'clock, my place?"

"I'm up to my ears in work right now—"

"You have to eat. Seven o'clock," he

repeated, with more firmness than Bev would have expected from a man who minced around in a pink Burberry scarf. "I'll cook my famous bucatini all'Amatriciana."

Whatever that was.

"It's pasta like you've never tasted before," he gushed, as if reading her mind. "With a light, spicy sauce made of pancetta, red pepper flakes, sun dried tomatoes and grated pecorino cheese. See you at seven."

At the other end of the connection, the entity posing as Allen Parker flipped his phone shut. Behind the rimless glasses he'd appropriated from Parker's corpse, his eyes gleamed with satisfaction.

Tonight, Kentar thought. Tonight he would confront the woman who'd caused him so much trouble.

It had taken him long enough to find her. He'd sent hunters as soon as he'd gotten wind that earthlings were searching for the medallion pieces hidden by the Pleiadian Council so many thousands of years ago.

After all his efforts to suppress development of the star navigator potential in earth women, he wasn't about to let them unlock the keys to developing that potential now.

Each of the hunters he'd sent to sabotage the search had failed. One had even gone over to the enemy. Rustam would pay dearly for his defection when Kentar caught up with him and the earth woman he now mated with.

As would this Beverly Ashton.

She, he'd discovered, was the driving force behind the search for the pieces of the medallion. The other woman, the professor, had deciphered the *Ad Astra* journals and developed her inherent ability to project through time and space. Carswell couldn't have done either, however, if Ashton hadn't provided the funding and the volunteers and the sheer muscle to keep the professor's experiments on track.

Kentar would crush them both, starting with this retired general. But first he would enjoy her.

His nostrils flared, and the coarse, residual hair of what was once a mane prickled all along his neck and upper spine. He could feel himself hardening, lengthening, until the urge to cover her, to subdue her, all but consumed him.

"Lord Kentar."

A starburst of energy from his control center in the Centaurian galaxy leaped into his head. He powered back a reply.

"Speak."

"We've received a signal. Hunter Third Rank Taikin thinks he may have stumbled across one of the searchers."

"Where?"

"At the court of the Chinese rulers, in earth year AD 674."

"Why does he think she's a searcher?"

"The male accompanying her claims she has special powers. And they both wear silver cuffs like those other searchers have worn."

By the stars! How had Carswell and Ashton managed to send another team so quickly? The last pair had escaped his hunter's clutches only weeks ago!

"Tell Taikin to watch her closely. If she leads him to the medallion piece and he takes possession of it, he has my permission to take possession of her, as well."

Astonishment rode on the next burst of energy.

"Do you mean…? He may breed her?"

It was an extraordinary concession. Only Kentar, as the alpha male of the vast Centaurian race, could breed at will. The lesser stallions required his permission to plant their seed, and he usually gave it only to those who had distinguished themselves in battle.

But Ashton and her crew had already recovered three sections of the medallion. He couldn't allow them to claim another.

"He may breed her…but only if she leads him to a piece of the medallion."

When Taikin received the signal, he almost tripped over his own feet.

"Ay yah!"

At his excited exclamation, the woman beside him glanced up in surprise. With a vicious effort of will, Taikin beat his jubilation into submission.

He was Tai Kin Su, he reminded himself fiercely. Planted at the Chinese court to keep watch on the empress, who had seized the reins of government against all odds. Powerful women like Wu Jao disrupted the natural order of things. Worse, their strength of will indicated they might well possess the starship navigator gene. For that reason Kentar had dispatched him to Wu Jao's court.

Unfortunately, Taikin had been forced to assume the form of a gelding in order to gain access to the inner workings of the imperial palace. But this female, this creature with the red hair and stubborn eyes, would provide him the means to revert to his Centaurian form at last.

If she led him to a piece of the medallion, he would go home a hero! He'd have his pick of broodmares. He could bask forever in his place in history.

He would take her with him, Tai decided. He hadn't felt so much as a stir of arousal since he'd arrived at this accursed court. But she... She piqued his interest as no woman had in longer than he could remember. Relishing the feeling, Tai escorted her through a maze of corridors and stopped in front of a red lacquered door.

"These apartments are always kept ready for visiting dignitaries. You will find them more than adequate."

"They have to be better than the dirt-floored cell I spent last night in," she murmured.

"See for yourself."

He lifted the latch and ushered her into a walled garden with an ornamental pond, a stone shrine with a statue of the goddess Guan Yin and pebbled walkways done in black-and-white designs.

Five interconnected chambers surrounded the small courtyard. One was a gathering area elegantly furnished with a low, black-lacquered table and cushions for eating, a couch for reclining and reading and a water clock that marked the twelve animals depicting each hour. The adjoining sleeping area contained a platform bed draped with rich furs and a tall, painted chest to store guests' belongings. Decorative scrolls embellished the walls and oiled rice paper covered the windows, to keep out the cold while letting in light.

The remaining chambers consisted of a kitchen with a ceramic stove for brewing tea, a bathing room and a small, windowless dormitory for the slaves assigned to the quarters. These appeared promptly, drawn by the sound of the courtyard gate slamming shut.

"You!"

At Tai's bark, a slight female in a Japanese-style kimono bobbed nervously. "Yes, Chief Eunuch?"

"Tell the slaves tending the bath fires to bring hot water. And you…"

He pointed to a second servant, this one clad in a short jacket and long gown.

"Go to the palace of the concubines. Tell

fourth-level concubine Jung Lo that Chief Eunuch Tai commands her to give you three sets of silk robes and undergarments. And slippers," he added, with a glance at Cassie's mud-and-snow-stained boots. "Two pairs."

When the maid scuttled away, Tai lifted his gaze to that of the searcher. He could see himself reflected in her emerald eyes. The prospect of mounting her made his excitement rise up and almost choke him.

"How are you called?"

"Cassandra, in my own land."

"What does it mean?"

Cassie barely contained a grimace.

In Greek mythology, Cassandra was the daughter of King Priam and Queen Hecuba of Troy. Because of her stunning beauty, Apollo lusted after her and tried to bribe her into his bed with the gift of prophecy. When she didn't yield to the god's advances, however, a furious Apollo decreed no one would ever believe her predictions.

Cassie's mother wasn't into Greek mythology. She'd just heard the name on a TV show and liked it. Talk about ironic twists of fate!

"It means seer," she informed Tai.

"It is too long," he said with a frown. "Too difficult to pronounce. I will call you Bo Fei."

"Spring Leaf?" she translated.

"Spring Leaf," Tai confirmed. "As your eyes are the color of mulberry leaves when they first open. Ah! Here is your bathwater."

"That was quick," Cassie murmured as a small army of servants trooped in with steaming buckets and marched across the courtyard.

"Hot water is always near at hand. You have only to ask. Come, we will rid you of those rags and cleanse you."

Ooo-kay, Cassie thought. No need to feel goosey about getting naked with a man for the second time in as many days. This one, at least, was harmless.

She accompanied him across the courtyard. When Tai slid open the door to the bathhouse, a billow of steam rolled out to envelope them both.

"Well, what do you know!" she exclaimed as she stepped inside. "Our own private sauna."

"I do not know this sauna," her escort said with a shrug, "but the bathing room is for use by you and the one who accompanies you, until the empress decrees otherwise."

Delighted, Cassie eyed the oval wooden tub occupying place of honor in the center of the chamber. Beside it was a low wooden platform with a stack of neatly folded bath sheets and an array of colorful bottles. On the other side of the tub, a square box held stones arranged in an artistic design around glowing coals.

"You!" Tai barked at the timid maid. "Ladle water onto the stones."

The girl leaped to do his bidding. More steam hissed and rose in clouds to surround the tub, which the other servants filled with hot water. Tai himself added a bucket of cold and tested the temperature before gesturing imperiously.

"Now, Spring Leaf, you may soak away the grime of your journey."

Cassie hesitated, but the muscle-bound eunuch didn't look as if he was going anywhere, and the idea of a bath was too, too tempting to resist. Not only did she carry the stink of camels, she still ached from her hours in the saddle. Peeling off her clothing, she sank to her neck in the warm water.

The little maid folded her legs and knelt beside the tub with liquid grace. "May I wash your hair?" she asked in her soft voice.

"Please." Sighing with pleasure, Cassie surrendered to the maid's nimble fingers. "What's your name?"

The girl looked at the eunuch for permission before replying.

"In my own tongue, my name means Unfolding Petals of White Peony. Here I am called simply Peony."

Tai was still there, watching with those keen dark eyes, when Cassie finished her bath. Reminding herself again that he was harmless, she rose from the tub wearing nothing but her armband and a satisfied smile. That slipped a little when Peony enfolded her in a drying sheet and Tai pushed the maid aside with a careless hand.

"Lie on the changing table," he instructed Cassie. "I will rub lotions into your skin."

"Isn't that a little below your pay grade?"

"I do not take your meaning."

She gestured to the maid standing with downcast eyes. "Shouldn't she perform such menial tasks instead of a chief eunuch?"

"She will, henceforth. Lie down."

Cassie was getting a little tired of having men throw that particular order at her. Still, she had to admit she wouldn't mind having this big, muscular male knead out the aches she hadn't quite soaked away.

She kept the sheet draped around her as she sat on the edge of the wooden platform and swung her legs onto it. She was barely face-down before Tai tugged the covering away.

"I have put my hands on women before," he drawled when she protested. "Many women."

"I bet you have. Just not this particular wo... Oooh!"

Warm oil splashed onto her shoulder blades. Tai's palms followed. Kneading, squeezing, stroking, he worked the kinks from her sore muscles.

"God, that feels good."

"It will feel better."

He dribbled more oil onto her spine. His strong fingers massaged her aching lower back before moving to the parts that had taken the worst beating from the wooden saddle. Her bottom, her thighs, her calves, even her ankles and toes got meticulous attention.

Cassie closed her eyes and gave herself up to the sheer ecstasy of his clever, clever hands. She could feel the tension seeping from her pores as he worked his way down one leg and up the other. Then his fingers slid between her thighs and she almost came off the table.

"Hey!"

"Be still."

Tai enforced the order by planting his free hand at the small of her back, pinning her to the table. His other hand probed the slick folds of flesh at her center.

"Unclench your legs," he urged. "Let me pleasure you like this…until I can pleasure you in other ways," he added in a rough whisper.

What other ways?

Cassie squirmed frantically. Was the guy going to pull a double-pronged dildo out of his sleeve? Or hitch her into one of those Chinese hanging basket contraptions? Or…

Who was she kidding? The man didn't need any additional instruments. His fingers pressed against her flesh, sending sensations shooting through her entire body. So intense she couldn't breathe. So wild she had to force herself to gather her muscles for a flip. If she made a quick half turn, she could deliver a swift kick to Big Guy's jaw.

She was going to do that. She really was! And she would have, if the door to the steamy bath chamber hadn't been yanked open at that moment.

"What the *hell!*"

The bellow was half astonishment, half outrage. Cassie twisted around and saw Max standing thunderstruck on the threshold. Two strides later, he'd crossed the room and had Tai by the throat.

The men were equally matched in size, but Max had the advantage of a couple of gallons of testosterone. With an animal growl, he slung the eunuch around and threw him through the open door.

Tai staggered into the walled courtyard, hit the lip of the ornamental pond and went in. He sat there in six inches of water, breathing fire as Max stalked toward him.

"Ma...uh, Lord Bro-dai!" Cassie grabbed the drying sheet and scrambled off the platform. "Wait!"

Max ignored her. Legs spread, one hand on his sword hilt, he looked ready to skewer the eunuch to a lily pad.

"I warned Inspector Li. Now I will warn you. Touch this woman again without my permission and you will lose what is left of your manhood."

"Spring Leaf is no longer your slave." The man's voice rose a full octave, squeaking with the force of his fury. "You gave her to the empress, and Her Heavenly Majesty charged me to make her presentable."

Max wrenched back his sleeve. His silver cuff flashed in the late-afternoon sunlight. "Until Her Heavenly Majesty accepts the slave and this cuff to control her, she is mine. You will not touch her again without my leave. Do you understand me?"

Tai gritted his teeth. "Yes."

"Address me with respect, eunuch."

Geesh! Brody was really getting into this "lord" business. Cassie might have admired his performance if the look in Tai's dark eyes hadn't promised dire retribution for this humiliation.

"Yes, Lord Bro-dai."

"Now leave us."

The eunuch dragged himself out of the pond. His silk robe dripped all the way to the red lacquered door.

"That was smart," Cassie said caustically, clutching the sheet to her oiled body with both hands. "Nothing like making a powerful enemy less than an hour after we get through the doors of the imperial palace!"

Max whirled on her. "Almost as smart as teaming up with a partner who can't keep—"

He broke off at the sight of the frightened face peeping around the door of the bath-house.

"Who are you?"

The maid's already pale cheeks drained of all color. "I…I am Peony."

"Why are you here?"

"I… I—"

"Speak, girl. I won't bite you."

The maid obviously had her doubts. With his bristling beard and wolf pelt, Max didn't exactly invite confidence.

"I am from the island of Hokkaido," she whispered fearfully. "I was given as part of the tribute my people pay each year to their Heavenly Majesties."

She edged around the door frame. With her hands tucked inside the sleeves of her kimono, she dipped her slender neck in a graceful bow.

"It is my duty to service those who occupy these chambers."

"Christ!" Max whipped his gaze back to Cassie. "Looks like we'll both enjoy this little sojourn, *Spring Leaf.*"

"Hey, wait a minute! You don't think Tai was, uh…"

"Servicing you?" His lip curled. "Sure looked like it from where I stood."

The fact that he'd pretty much hit it on the mark didn't score him any points with Cassie.

"I won't dignify that with a response," she said, chin high. "Nor will I continue this discussion here in the courtyard. It's cold, and I'm not dressed."

"So I see."

His gray eyes burned a scorch mark at every point where the damp sheet clung to her skin.

"We'll take this inside," she declared, flipping back her wet hair. "Peony, will you please brew us a pot of tea?"

The girl looked profoundly relieved to be

released from the presence of such fierce outlanders. With another frightened glance at Max, she bobbed her head.

"Yes, mistress. I have a pot of Blue Lotus steeping in the kitchen. They have brought you clothes," she added hesitantly. "Silk robes and embroidered slippers and a pair of wooden clogs so you may walk in the garden, if you wish it. Shall I help you to dress before I serve tea?"

"Good idea."

Cassie started after Peony and tossed Max a nasty look over one shoulder. "While I'm getting dressed, you might want to give the sauna a try. Maybe you can steam away some of your stink…and some of the dirt in your mind."

Chapter 6

The woman with no talent is one who has merit.

—Confucius

His mind? She thought he should wash the dirt from *his* mind?

Max stalked into the bath chamber, fuming, and sent the bathhouse door slamming against its uprights. He would need more than a tub of hot water and clouds of hissing steam to wash away the image of his jump partner stretched across that low platform. Buck naked. With Big Hands groping between her thighs.

He should have wrung the bastard's throat. He might yet, and Cassie's, too! What was she thinking, stripping down to the buff in front of Tai? The man might not be able to get it up anymore, but he certainly remembered what lust felt like. That was evident from his heavy-eyed leer when he'd had his hands on Cassie.

Swearing, Max threw the wolf pelt at the floor and unbuckled his sword belt. The scene he'd stumbled on was seared into his mind. All he could see was Cassie's long, slender body. The curve of her calves. Those rounded buttocks and her smooth, sloping back, glistening with oil.

What disgusted him more than anything else, though, was the undeniable fact that he'd been looking forward to rubbing her down himself.

"Dammit!"

He kicked off his boots, then yanked his woolen tunic over his head. When his loosely woven undergarments joined the heap on the floor, he had to fold his knees almost to his chin to fit into the oval tub, still filled with sudsy water. Scowling, he used both hands to scoop up the tepid liquid and splash it over his face and shoulders.

Was this what Cassie had done to Jerry Holland? he wondered savagely. Wormed her way into his head? Made him ache with wanting her, until all he could think about was sliding his hands over those smooth flanks and sinking into her wet, hot flesh?

If she had, it was no surprise their last mission had turned into disaster. He still wasn't sure about this bet she'd told him about, or how it had played in Jerry's death, but Max did know one thing with absolute certainty. He would not let the growing hunger Cassandra Jones roused in him sabotage *this* mission.

With that grim vow, he yanked the leather tie from his hair and grabbed a bottle of what looked like liquid soap. He grimaced at the flowery scent, but dumped the stuff on top of his head. He'd just worked up a good lather when the door to the bathhouse opened.

It closed with a bang and the maid rushed inside, her expression horrified. "Master! Please to let me bathe you!"

"No, thanks."

"It is my duty."

"I can manage."

She wrung her hands, looking as if she was about to burst into tears. "I…I am so sorry my humble self does not please you."

"Your humble self is fine. I just don't need any help."

"I understand," she sniffed. "I most earnestly beg the master's pardon." Shoulders slumping, she shuffled in small, dejected steps toward the door. "This unworthy slave most richly deserves the whipping she will receive when she goes to Chief Eunuch Tai and begs him to send another to tend you."

Well, hell!

"Wait," Max called gruffly. "How about

you bring some clean water for me to rinse off with?"

She beamed a relieved smile. "Yes, master!"

Her duties didn't end with the rinse water. Before Max knew it, she was stropping a straight razor to shave away his scratchy beard. Then, somehow, he ended up stretched out on the wooden platform while Peony's nimble fingers worked magic on his naked body.

"Thanks," he muttered when she'd finished.

"I sent for fresh garments for you," she said shyly. "Please to let me help you dress."

The garments consisted of loose drawers, baggy riding trousers that tucked into his boots and a military-style tunic of fine silk. A padded jacket with elaborate frogs and winged epaulets provided warmth. Feeling human again, Max joined Cassie in the sitting room.

She was seated on a cushion at the low, square table. When he entered, she glanced up and raised a brow. "Nice getup."

"You, too."

Like him, she was dressed in Chinese attire. While Peony was working on him in the bathhouse, someone had brushed her auburn hair to a lustrous sheen and piled it on top of her head in an intricate series of braids and swirls. The style showed off her slender neck and a soft feathering of curls that brushed the collar of her beautifully embroidered turquoise jacket. But it was the translucent silk gown she wore beneath the jacket that had Max doing a quick double take. The shimmering pink gown was styled low in front. So low Max's palms started to sweat.

She'd also been laced into some kind of undergarment—the ancient version of a corset, he guessed. The tight fabric mounded her breasts and offered him a tantalizing view of the valley between.

"Do you want some tea?"

He wrenched his gaze upward. "Huh?"

"Tea. Do you want some?"

Nodding, he folded his legs and sank onto the cushion opposite hers. With his skin still tingling from his massage, he felt compelled to offer a gruff apology.

"Look, I may have overreacted about that business with Tai."

"You think?"

"Yeah, well… For a guy who's been clipped, ole Tai sure seemed to enjoy having his hands on you."

She poured a pale stream into a thimble-size porcelain cup and passed it to him. "That little incident kind of weirded me out," she admitted reluctantly. "But I've been mulling it over."

Red seeped into her cheeks. Fiddling with her teacup, she mumbled an explanation. "I think palace eunuchs are trained to, you know, pleasure wives and concubines. It's either that, or the women have to pleasure themselves. There are so many of them, they may get called to their master's bed only once or twice a year. If then."

That was true enough. Max knew Chinese law allowed a man only one wife, but as many concubines as he could afford to maintain. Great for the guy. Not so great for his harem.

He also knew there was no shame in becoming a concubine. Especially a royal one. Families considered it a great boone if their daughter was accepted into the emperor's household. If she won his favor, she could send wealth and honors their way.

"Didn't our mission prebrief indicate Wu Jao was one of five or six hundred concubines before she worked her way up to wife, then empress?"

"More like a thousand," Cassie replied. "She got rid of a bunch of them after she came to power, though. And speaking of Wu Jao…" His partner took a swig of tea and eyed him over the rim of her cup. "You want to tell me what went on between you two after I departed the scene?"

"Not much. She asked about where we came from and how we had traveled to Chang'an. Then she invited me to join her at a small banquet tonight in her private chambers."

"Max!" Cassie jolted straight up in her chair, her eyes wide with alarm. "You have to be careful! Tai told me the empress has strong sexual appetites. He said, too, there are all kinds of rumors circulating about our girl, but no man who ever got between the sheets with her would live long enough to confirm them."

"Thanks," he drawled. "Just what I needed to hear."

"It's a matter of legitimacy," Cassie insisted. "Although Jao is the real power behind the throne, she can't appear to be unfaithful to her husband or the warlords will challenge her sons' right to inherit after her." Cassie chewed on her lower lip, her eyes worried. "If she tries to move on you, you'll just have to keep her dangling until we find the medallion."

"Right. Any suggestions on how to accomplish that?"

"I don't know. Maybe…" Frowning, she drummed her fingers on the tabletop. When she glanced up, her gaze snagged on the emergency signal cuff banding his wrist.

"Maybe you could link your sexual prowess to the ESC. You told the empress that's how you control me. You could explain that it takes every ounce of your energy to restrain and direct mine."

"It might work," he said slowly. "But only until you've demonstrated your skills. Once she accepts the gift I've brought her, I'll have to hand over my cuff at the same time I hand you over."

"We'll worry about that when it happens. Right now our major concern is keeping you in Wu's sights but out of her bed until we get a fix on the medallion."

Max couldn't help it. He burst out laughing.

"What?" Cassie demanded.

"I'm supposed to be your guardian-slash-watchdog," he reminded her, grinning. "Quite a switch having you scheme to protect *me* from the evil empress."

"You'd better hope this scheme works, Bubba, or you'll be singing soprano with Tai. At best. At worst, you'll end up in a vat of boiling oil."

"And on that cheerful note…" He shoved back his chair. "I'd better find the servant who's supposed to escort me to the empress's private apartments."

Cassie rose and accompanied him to the door to the courtyard. Her expression troubled, she laid a hand on his arm.

"Be careful, okay?"

Manfully, Max kept his gaze from dropping to her hand, with an intermediate stop in the vicinity of her breasts.

"I will. In the meantime, you'd better dig into your bag of tricks and conjure up some weather mojo for Her Heavenly Majesty."

Just moments after Max departed, Peony appeared at the head of a small army of servants. They trooped in with an array of delicate porcelain bowls filled with everything from hot barley soup to sugared pine nuts.

"Please to eat," the maid said softly, setting ivory chopsticks and a porcelain spoon on a woven place mat.

Cassie was too nervous about Max and the empress to do more than nibble at some wheat noodles and spiced pork. His reminder that she had to conjure up some weather mojo didn't do much for her appetite, either. Waving away the rest of the dishes, she pulled on an embroidered jacket stuffed with goose down, shoved her feet into wooden clogs and went out into the walled court-yard.

She'd studied the topography, climatology and weather patterns of ancient Chang'an—modern-day Xi'an—in exhaustive detail during her mission prep. She knew the city enjoyed a full range of seasons. Warm, moist summers with the wind blowing from the south. Mild springs and autumns. Cold, dry winters with northerly winds. Not much snow, even during the coldest months of the year, when the average daily temperature hovered around 40° F.

Average, of course, being the critical factor.

An Arctic blast could sweep down from

the mountains with little warning. Wind and rain could roar up from the south with monsoon force. If Cassie missed the signs... If she ignored nature's subtle warnings, as she had on her last mission with Jerry...

The spicy pork she'd just eaten churned in her stomach. Her life wasn't the only one hanging on her instincts. Max was in this with her. The team back at the lab was counting on them both. Failure wasn't an option.

Yet she couldn't keep the crippling doubts at bay. They haunted her as she prowled the courtyard, artfully illuminated now with flickering lanterns, and searched for nature's clues.

The high walls gave her only a tiny patch of sky to work with, and blocked any attempt to measure wind direction or velocity. The ornamental pond, unfortunately, was too shallow to adequately assess evaporation level.

That left the plants dotting the garden. The glossy-leafed rhododendron showed plump white berries and the needles of the weeping yew arching over the stone shrine felt moist to the touch. Cassie didn't know if that was because it had stored up recent rainfall, though, or because palace gardeners watered the garden regularly. Then she spotted a small white clump high in the yew's branches.

Yes! A rain star fungus. It opened into a filmy web to catch moisture, and scrunched into a tight wad in dry weather. This one was closed up, which suggested no imminent change in precipitation levels.

Cassie would check it again tomorrow. She would also have to get a good look at the clouds and observe the smoke rising from chimneys before making any kind of prediction as to winds or temperature. But at least now she had *something* to work with.

"Mistress!" Peony peered at her from the door to the living area. "It is cold. Please to come in and allow me to prepare you for the master."

"Excuse me?"

"We must harmonize your five colors before Lord Bro-dai returns."

At Cassie's blank look, the maid clicked her tongue and herded her toward the sleeping chamber.

"Your hair and lips are a most harmonious red, so I do not need to apply rouge, but we must whiten your throat and paint your nipples."

"My nipples? I don't think so."

"The paint contains the fur of deer antler ground to a fine powder," the maid explained earnestly. "It is a most potent stimulant. When the master suckles your breast, much blood will flow to his jade stalk and he will give you the prescribed seven consistencies."

The idea of Max suckling her anything sent heat spearing through Cassie's belly. It flamed even hotter at the idea of experiencing the seven prescribed yin orgasms before he poured out his yang.

Gulping, she suppressed the erotic images and shook her head. "You've got the wrong idea, Peony. I don't, uh, ride his jade stalk."

Surprise stopped the maid in midstep. "Why do you not? I observed it this afternoon, when I massaged him. It has a most prodigious length and girth. Surely it would take you to the highest levels of joyous benefit."

Ha! So Cassie wasn't the only one who'd gotten a rubdown in the bathhouse this afternoon. Interesting that Brody hadn't shared that bit of information!

"Thanks, anyway," she told the maid, "but my colors don't need harmonizing."

"Please, mistress." A look of distress flickered across Peony's face. "It is my duty to prepare you."

"Not tonight."

"Ah, so." She hung her head. Her shoulders slumped. "You do not think I am skilled enough to enhance your womanly essence," she said in a small voice. "I will go to…"

A violent shudder racked her.

"I will go to Chief Eunuch Tai and beg him to send you a more worthy maid."

"You don't have to go to Tai. We'll just keep this between us girls."

"You don't understand," Peony whispered, glancing over her shoulder. "There are spies everywhere. The very walls have ears. If I shirk my duty, Chief Eunuch Tai will hear of it and have me whipped. As he should," she added bravely, blinking back tears.

Cassie caved. A little ground-up antler fur on her nipples wasn't worth a whipping.

"All right, already. Go get your paint."

Breaking into a grateful smile, the maid gestured to the sleeping platform. "Please to sit while I fetch paints and unguents."

"I didn't agree to unguents. Peony! No unguents!"

She should have saved her breath. The maid scuttled out and returned with two helpers and an array of bottles and brushes that would have sent a supermodel into throes of ecstasy. She also carried a razor and a pot of creamy shaving lotion.

Spies or not, Cassie drew the line at having her pubic hair removed. Peony pleaded and went the teary-eyed route again, but Cassie finally convinced her that the harmonious red at the juncture of her thighs signified good luck. Looking doubtful, the maid signaled her helpers to hand her the paint pots.

A half hour later, Cassie was painted and perfumed and sporting a narrow, exquisitely embroidered belly cloth that tied loosely around her hips. Its fringed ends just brushed her pubic mound.

"I see now mistress speaks the truth!" Peony exclaimed as she adjusted the belly band's drape. "The red of your womanhood hints at the heat within. Surely such a heavenly furnace will stoke the master's fire."

"It better not," Cassie muttered as two other servants draped a diaphanous nightdress of celery-colored silk over her head.

As soon as the silk slithered over her hips, she saw the gown wasn't just diaphanous. The damned thing was completely transparent.

"I need a warmer nightdress," she protested. "I'll freeze in this."

Peony tsked and gestured to the furs scattered across the sleeping platform. "They will keep you warm. Until the master arrives," she added slyly.

After the other servants had folded Cassie's daytime garments and put them in the chest, Peony shooed them away and departed with a final request. "Please to use neck rest. You do not wish to disturb beauteous arrangement of hair."

Lips pursed, Cassie eyed the curved neck supports positioned at the head of the sleeping platform. Last night she'd had a dirt floor and Max to keep her warm. Tonight it was a wooden block for her neck and rich furs. Until Max returned from his tête-à-tête with the empress, that was.

If he returned.

He would, she thought fiercely. He had to. He couldn't risk getting too intimate with Wu Jao. Not while they still had no clue as to the whereabouts of the medallion. Until they did, Max had damn well better crawl into bed here. With Cassie.

To her disgust, the thought made her

painted nipples get tight and tingly. They popped to attention, two stiff little soldiers poking at the celery silk, while her heavenly furnace fired up.

Okay! All right! She'd sworn off all men since the disaster with Jerry Holland, but she was only human. She couldn't control her instinctive responses to the thought of lying next to Max's hard, muscled body. She *could,* however, ignore them.

Determined to do just that, she eased down, found a comfortable angle on the wooden headrest and dragged the soft furs over her.

"Has anyone ever told you how beautiful you are?"

Bev Ashton glanced up in surprise to find Allen Parker studying her over the rim of his brandy snifter.

"Not lately," she replied dryly.

This had to be the strangest ending to the strangest night of her life. She'd trudged through the frost-tipped desert landscaping separating her condo from Parker's almost five hours ago. She'd planned to scarf down his bucatini à la whatever, plead the excuse of heavy work and then leave.

To her surprise, Parker had proved a wonderful host. Amusing and astonishingly well read and only mildly swishy. Even more disconcerting, his swishiness seemed to diminish with each passing hour.

"Your cheekbones," he murmured as his gaze roamed her face. "So high and proud. Like Marie Antoinette's."

When Bev gave a small snort, he smiled.

"There's a rather magnificent painting of her in the Gold Salon at Versailles. Perhaps you've seen it."

"No, I haven't."

"Poor Marie," he mused. "She was such a vain, stupid woman. Your exact opposite."

The compliment gave Bev a dart of unexpected and completely irrational pleasure. For heaven's sake! She was long past the age of being susceptible to a little flattery.

Or not, she discovered when Parker lifted

his brandy snifter in a salute. His eyes were as admiring as they were intense.

"Like this vintage Armagnac, some women only improve with age."

"That," Bev replied, pushing out of her chair, "is my cue to depart the premises before you find out differently."

Kentar surged to his feet. Instinct bred into him from generations of alpha stallions would allow no female to escape before he was done with her. Just in time he controlled the raw urge to dominate and subdue.

He'd derived a vicious satisfaction from playing with General Beverly Ashton tonight. She thought she could defeat him. She, and this professor who had learned to harness the sine waves, thought they could retrieve all twelve pieces of the medallion and effect Earth's entry into the Pleiadian Council.

They would fail. But first Kentar would rouse everything that was female in this general, this commander of men. Then, and only then, would he show her what it meant to be mounted by a real male.

With a deliberate sway of his hips, he retrieved her coat from the hall closet and almost laughed out loud when he turned to catch her rolling her eyes.

"Good night, Beverly."

"'Night, Allen. Thanks again for dinner."

"My pleasure."

He held out her coat. When she angled to the side to thrust an arm in a sleeve, Kentar nuzzled her neck and concentrated all his force.

She twisted away and looked up, startled. Her obvious confusion gave him immense pleasure. Riding its crest, he released his force and let it pour from him like a powerful ejaculation.

The energy rolled over her in dark waves. Her lips parted. Heat rose like a crimson tide in her cheeks. Her breath shortened to gasps.

Kentar didn't bring her to pleasure. It was enough that she pleasured him. Reining in his force, he opened the front door.

"We'll do this again," he promised with an unctuous smile. "Soon."

Bev walked back to her condo in a daze. She couldn't figure out what had just happened. If she didn't know better, she could swear Allen Parker had almost treated her to a mental orgasm.

Allen Parker, of all people!

Either she was in more need of a hot, young stud than she thought or she was losing her judgment when it came to the male of the species. Or…

Her stomach knotted as another possibility burst like a mortar round inside her head.

Good God! Was it possible? Could effete, pretty-boy Parker be one of the Centaurian sent to this planet to control its women?

The notion was absurd! Where were the bulging muscles? The powerful haunches of an alpha stallion?

Then again, what better way to get past Bev's guard than to shimmy up to her like a playful gelding! Except that nip on the neck hadn't been exactly playful. Her skin still tingled where his teeth had scraped it.

Her jaw tight, she reached into her coat

pocket for her cell phone and punched the lab's speed-dial button. The officer on the watch answered on the second ring.

"Yes, ma'am."

"Get on the lab's computers. Pull up everything you can on Allen Parker, age approximately thirty-five, hair light brown. He lives next door to me."

"Yes, ma'am."

Chapter 7

Women's nature is passive.
                                    —Confucius

Cassie lay with her neck cradled on wood
as late evening deepened into night.

She heard Peony murmuring to the other
servants and the low clink of dishes being
cleared from the other room. The oil lamp on
the lacquered chest across from the sleeping
platform flickered with a dim light. Some-

where in the maze of corridors outside, a door slammed. She dragged the soft furs up to her chin, sure she would remain a tight bundle of nerves until Max returned from his session with the empress.

The next thing she heard was the raucous crow of a rooster. She blinked her eyes open, shocked to see light flooding the sleeping chamber. Even more disconcerting, her head rested on something that didn't feel anything like wood.

She had to admit Max's shoulder was a lot more comfortable than the neck rest. She tilted her head, wincing when her complicated arrangement of braids and loops tugged at her scalp, and studied the profile only inches away.

His jaw, cleanly shaved the afternoon before, had sprouted bristles. They glinted the same tawny gold as his hair and lashes in the bright light of morning. If he'd spent the previous night in sin and dissipation with the empress, it didn't show when those golden lashes lifted and his gray eyes met hers.

"'Bout time you woke up, Jones."

She shoved a lopsided braid out of her face and thrust herself off his shoulder. Propped on one elbow, she demanded, "What happened last night?"

"Turns out I was the guest of honor at a private banquet for fifteen or so women and men."

Cassie's stomach knotted. She was envisioning a wild orgy when Max relieved her mind.

"The empress seated me between the general who commands the palace guards and Princess Mei Yin, her oldest daughter. Inspector Li was there, too. There was a lot of talking, a lot of eating, some poetry reading and this really graceful dancer from Thailand, or whatever it's called in this century. I actually had a pretty good time."

"What about the medallion? Did you see any bronze pieces depicting various constellations?"

"Not a one. The only zodiac signs I saw were those from the Chinese calendar. The dog, the sheep, the rat, the ox and so on. Those were everywhere."

Cassie hadn't thought it would be that easy. Still, she had to swallow a lump of bitter disappointment as Max continued.

"They wanted to know about the land I come from. And about you, of course. They're all anxious to see you do your thing today." His gaze sharpened. "You up for it?"

"I have to get outside the palace first. I can't get a fix on wind direction or velocity inside these walls."

"Not a problem. The general invited me to watch the guards perform a mounted drill this morning. It takes place on a parade field just outside the palace gates. The empress will be there, too, and commanded me to bring you."

"When?"

"At the hour of the snake."

"That's, like, 9:00 a.m.!" Cassie threw off the downy silk comforter, her mind racing. "Before we go, I need to see if the pond surface froze last night and check this yew tree in the garden to—"

"What the heck is that?"

"What?"

"On the front of your gown?"

She glanced down and made a face. Two large brown smears stained the front of the celery-green silk.

"Ground-up antler fuzz."

"You're kidding, right?"

"I wish."

She scrambled off the sleeping platform. This wasn't the time to explain.

Max's low whistle reminded her the gown wasn't only stained, it was completely transparent. Cassie threw him a nasty glance as she stalked toward the painted chest.

"Do you mind?"

"Not at all," he drawled, crossing his arms behind his head for a better view.

Scowling, she yanked the chest's brass latch, dragged out an armful of clothing and shoved her feet into the wooden clogs. The thud of her footsteps on the pebbled path to the bathhouse brought Peony darting out of the servants' room. Hastily tying the sash of her kimono, she tripped after Cassie.

"Mistress is up very early."

"I need to pee."

"What is this pee?"

"Make water. Urinate."

"Ah, so! Why do you not use the slop jar under the sleeping platform? It is of the finest porcelain and we empty it regularly."

"I left the slop jar for the, uh, master."

Damn! She would have to try harder not to gag over that word.

"Isn't there another jar in the bathhouse?"

"Of course, mistress. Will you dress there, too?" Peony asked, eyeing the bundle in Cassie's arms.

"Yes."

The maid looked a little shocked at this breach of protocol, but said only that she would bring her pots of paint to the bathhouse, along with mint tea to freshen the mouth.

"And a comb," Cassie called after her. "These braids have to go."

She'd had plenty of time to think about her

command performance while Max was out carousing last night. She was supposed to be a Celtic princess. She'd arrived at the palace in the soiled garments of a slave, and she certainly wouldn't create any special mystique by aping Chinese hairstyle and dress. She needed her own look.

She had it set in her mind when Peony returned with her pots and a styling comb. "Never mind the paint. How many pairs of riding trousers did you bring Lord Brody?"

"Three, mistress."

"Please, go fetch me a pair."

"Do you think to dress like a woman of Lo-Shun?"

Cassie had no idea who the heck Lo-Shun women were or how they dressed, but took heart from the fact that Peony was more curious than shocked.

"I think to dress like a woman of my own land. Hurry. I must be ready by the hour of the snake."

The maid returned with a pair of baggy black trousers and watched dubiously while

Cassie used the pointed end of the comb to pick apart the cuffs banding each full leg. She then proceeded to rip one sleeve from a padded jacket of embroidered, jade-green silk.

Peony protested this desecration with a small shriek. "Mistress!"

"I must display the symbol of my power."

And be able to get to it, like, *fast* if things got dicey.

Her silver armband flashing, Cassie shrugged into the jacket, pulled up the now wide-legged trousers and secured both by wrapping the red silk belly band from the night before around her waist.

"There." Smoothing the fringed belt, she took a few experimental steps. "This is what we call a riding skirt in my land."

"But your left arm is bare. You will take a fever from the cold! And your hair," Peony moaned as Cassie attacked the braids. "That was the Four Waterfalls arrangement, made popular by Princess Shih, of the house of Chang."

"Not to worry. I'm going to show you a style made popular by Princess Angelina Jolie, of my tribe."

When Cassie strode back into the sitting area, Max did a double take.

The bedraggled slave of the day before had disappeared. So had the painted courtesan who'd almost made him swallow his tongue this morning. This Cassie looked every inch the powerful seer from distant lands.

Her hair was brushed back from her temples and caught with a cloisonné comb before rippling to her shoulders in fiery waves. The quartz crystal in her armband winked a half dozen colors in the bright sunlight. She stood tall, almost arrogant, in a silk, one-sleeved jacket that deepened the green of her eyes.

"You going to be warm enough in that?"

"Half of me will."

"If the other half gets cold, lean into me. Want some breakfast before we go?" he asked, nodding to the bowls on the lacquered table.

She downed a gulp of tea and was spearing her chopsticks at fried dumplings dribbled with honey when Max went into the sleeping chamber to retrieve his sword. He belted it on, slung the wolf pelt over his shoulders and returned.

"You've got honey on your lip," he stated, jerking his chin in her direction.

When her tongue darted out to snag the glistening drop, the punch to Max's gut hit without warning. He stood there, watching her tongue make a slow circuit of her lips, battling the almost overwhelming urge to trace the wet trail with his thumb, his teeth, his own tongue.

Then she looked up and caught him staring. Their eyes locked. The muffled sounds of the palace faded. For a crazy moment it was just the two of them, dropped together into an unfamiliar world, bound by their mission and the knowledge that they needed each other to make it back to their own century alive.

"Cassie…"

"Yes?"

Max stifled the urge to tell her to err on the side of caution in her predictions. She knew the penalties for failure as well as he did.

"Good luck."

"Thanks." She gave him a shaky smile and squared her shoulders. "Let's do it."

Before leaving their assigned quarters, Cassie checked the lily pond and the yew. The pond's surface was smooth and still, with only a thin rim of ice around the edges that didn't tell her anything. The tight clump of fungus high up in the yew's branches, however, appeared to have loosened. Not much. Just enough to kick Cassie's pulse up a notch.

They found Inspector Li in the outer court-yard, already mounted on his muscular Three Rivers–bred gelding. Li's topknot seemed to pull his perpetual sneer even tighter as he took in Cassie's one-sleeved jacket.

"Do you think to ape the ways of the

women of Lo-Shun? If so, you must cut off your right breast so you may draw a bow more easily."

Good Lord! Were those legends that had been passed down through the ages about Amazons true? Could descendants of the fierce female warriors described by the Greek historian Herodotus be alive and kicking here in ancient China? Cassie sincerely hoped she got to meet one before she and Max departed the seventh century.

"Mount," Li ordered brusquely. "We are to join the empress's cavalcade at the eastern gate."

Shivers of anticipation, excitement and sheer nerves danced along Cassie's bare arm as she gathered her protesting muscles and swung into the saddle. Her nervousness tripled when they joined the empress's elaborate entourage.

Wu Jao rode in a magnificent litter carried on the shoulders of twelve uniformed bearers. The conveyance was lacquered in red and the royal yellow, richly ornamented and so heavily gilded it seemed to be made primarily of gold. The silk curtains had been rolled up so the empress could enjoy the sight of her subjects prostrating themselves in the dirt as she was carried by.

To protect her heavenly countenance from being ogled, she wore a flat black hat that reminded Cassie of a high-school graduation mortarboard. This one had strings of lustrous pearls and jade beads hanging from the front and back edges, though, forming jeweled curtains. With the hat she wore a sumptuous silk cloak trimmed in ermine.

Two of her sons and a daughter had joined her for the outing. The princes were mounted on magnificent golden stallions. Their sister, the beautiful Princess Mei Yin, lounged in a litter almost as ornate as that of the empress.

Preceded by acrobats and jugglers, and drummers hammering great bronze gongs, the flamboyant procession started off. It provided such a banquet for the senses that Cassie had to force her mind to shut out the color and noise and focus instead on the small things around her.

Like the smoke from joss sticks stuck in pots of sand outside street temples. She took careful note of the way it angled lazily instead of curling straight up.

And when the procession approached the bird market with its hundreds of stalls crammed with wicker cages, she strained to listen to the shrill whistles and chirps.

As a child Cassie had always sensed that sounds were sharper before a storm, but she didn't know why until she studied meteorology in college. There she'd learned that sound waves travel upward and outward into the atmosphere during fair weather. A low pressure system, however, bent those waves back to the earth and made sounds seem sharper, louder. She wasn't completely sure, but she *thought* the bird calls sounded louder this morning than they had when she and Max had ridden past the same market on their way into the city.

The signs were adding up, she told herself

in a desperate attempt to steady her nerves. The rain star fungus. The smoke rising at an angle. The bird trills.

She couldn't shake the doubts that had plagued her since Jerry Holland's death, though, until the procession passed through the eastern gates and she got a glimpse of the high mountain pass they'd descended from yesterday. Her heart thumping, she edged her mount closer to Max's.

"Max! Look at the mountains."

Eyes narrowing, he skimmed the snow-capped peaks. "What am I looking for?"

"Do they seem closer?"

"Closer than what?"

"Than they looked yesterday," she said impatiently, "when we entered the city."

"I don't know. Maybe a little. Not as hazy, anyway."

"Yes!"

"Okay, Spring Leaf, clue me in here."

"I'm pretty sure we have a low pressure front approaching. The heavier air in a front pushes dust particles to the ground and clears the air, making distant objects appear more in focus."

Max nodded but seemed hung up on the "pretty sure" portion of her comment. "Do you feel confident enough to estimate when this front will arrive?"

"Not until we pass beyond the city walls and I get a good look at the sky to the west and south."

Despite hedging her bets, Cassie now felt close to seventy percent certainty. That nudged to a ninety-nine-point-nine when the procession mounted a small rise to the parade ground. Imperial guards in burnished armor ringed the field, their spears crossed. Colorful banners fluttered from the royal pavilion positioned for prime viewing midfield.

As the cavalcade followed the empress's litter toward the pavilion, Cassie scanned the vista behind her.

"Look." Pointing at the sky to the south, she chanted happily, "'Mares' tails and mackerel scales make tall ships take in their sails.'"

Max craned around to follow her pointing finger.

"Sailors used to call those wispy white streaks blowing up from the south mares' tails," she told him. "They're cirrus clouds and generally indicate the approach of an upper air disturbance, usually within the next twelve to twenty-four hours. If they build into altocumulus—flat gray clumps of clouds that sailors thought resembled fish scales—we're in for some really rough weather."

The glint of approval in Max's eyes almost made up for Inspector Li's glower when they dismounted and a soldier marched up to Max.

"Most Heavenly Empress wishes you to sit with her to watch the drill. You are to bring the sorceress with you."

Cassie's confidence took a sudden nose-dive but she kept her chin high as she and Max edged through the crowd of courtiers surrounding the royal pavilion. The empress sat under the colorful canopy in a thronelike chair. A considerably less elegant chair stood vacant beside her. Her sons and Princess Mei Yin were seated behind their mother, on a raised dais with the lesser nobles. The remaining courtiers stood in groups flanking the pavilion.

Looking like a beautiful porcelain doll under her elaborate headdress, Jao flicked her doelike eyes over Cassie before turning to Max. "So, Lord Bro-dai. I see your seer has bathed and robed herself in a most peculiar fashion."

"She has indeed, most beautiful and gracious queen."

"How is she called?"

"Cassandra in her own land. It has been suggested Spring Leaf may suit her in this land."

"Spring Leaf." Jao shifted her gaze to Cassie again. "Yes, I see the new, bright green in her eyes. Tell me, Spring Leaf, what change do you foretell in the weather?"

"I foretell rain, Your Majesty. It comes from the south."

"Humph." Someone in the crowd of courtiers openly scoffed.

Lifting a delicately painted brow, Jao singled out a slight gentleman with a long gray beard and a richly embroidered cap covering his topknot. He wore the simple blue gown and padded jacket of a scholar, but the glowing ruby button on his cap signified he held a high rank.

"You disagree, Lord Sing?"

The man stepped forward and prostrated himself. "No, Most Heavenly Majesty. I merely beg leave to question this as the pronouncement of a great seer, as rain comes from the south more often than it does not."

"True. Rise, Chief Astrologer, and question her yourself."

Cassie's stomach cramped into a tight knot. Astrology was an old and greatly revered science in China. The ancients' measurements of the heavens were so precise that their calendar accounted for anomalies like leap years, and counted the months, days and hours down to the minute. Every major event, from planting the first seed of the spring to launching a warship, was predicated on the knowledge of seasons and tides held by learned men like this one.

"You say it will rain, outlander." Stroking his beard with a gnarled hand, the court astrologer pinned Cassie with a hard stare. "When?"

She threw another glance at the sky to the south and felt the breeze on her face. The wind was freshening. She was sure it was freshening.

"Rain will come before the hour of the goat, most revered shaman."

The astrologer stared into her eyes for long moments. Then slowly, so slowly, he turned to the empress.

"She has the gift, Most Heavenly Majesty. I, too, predict rain by that hour."

"Do you indeed? Well, we shall see." With a casual wave of one hand, Wu Jao dismissed the astrologer. "Lord Bro-dai, you may sit beside me. Your seer may sit at our feet."

Max performed severe mental gyrations for the next hour.

Cassie leaned her bare arm into his trousered leg for warmth, saying nothing, while he divided his attention between the empress, the clouds to the south and the astounding precision of the mounted riders. Each cavalry drill was an exercise in superb horsemanship, every chariot charge a spectacle of skill and daring.

The mounted archers put on one of the most amazing shows. Astride matched sorrel horses, a squad of some forty or so wheeled onto the parade ground. At a signal from their captain, the first twenty spurred their mounts. When they were midfield and moving at full gallop, their captain shouted a command to the drummer riding beside him. "Draw!"

The drummer beat a wooden mallet once against a silver gong. The sound was high and thin, so it could be heard in battle over the thunder of pounding hooves. With astounding precision, the twenty rose up in their stirrups, whipped arrows from their quivers, notched them and drew their bow-strings.

"Release!"

The drummer banged the gong twice. A rain of lethal missiles flew toward straw targets at the far end of the field. When every one hit dead center, the spectators burst into wild applause and the empress signaled her approval with a benign smile.

The first squad had barely cleared the field when the second squad began their run. They reached the release point at midfield, their captain gave his command and the archers drew their bows.

Afterward Max would swear everything happened in slow motion from that point. He saw one of the horses stumble, heard the crowd gasp. The rider was already up in the stirrups, an arrow notched and drawn. His mount's violent maneuvers as it tried to recover threw the archer sideways in the saddle. His arrow launched, soaring high into the air before beginning a lethal downward arc.

Max saw its trajectory, realized it would hit the royal pavilion and had less than a second to react. Shoving Cassie clear of the arrow's path, he lunged for the empress. His dive toppled her chair and took them both down just as the arrow tore through the canopy and thudded into the platform.

There was a second or two of stunned silence from the spectators before chaos erupted. Princess Mei Yin screamed. The courtiers shouted in panic. The elite imperial guards leaped forward, their pikes shoulder high and aimed for Max. He figured he was dead meat until the empress twisted out from under him and flung up an arm.

"Hold!"

Max pushed to his feet and reached down for her. She'd lost her hat with its beaded veil, and her face was red with fury. Then she spotted the arrow. Its tip was buried in the platform a scant inch from where she'd been sitting.

The color drained from Jao's cheeks. Whirling, she hissed out a command. The archer who'd fired the missile had already been dragged off his horse. At her command, he was shoved to his knees and beheaded on the spot. His body had barely thudded to the dirt when his disgraced captain turned his bloody sword blade up and fell on it.

The general who'd arranged the exhibition wasn't spared Wu Jao's wrath, either. He stepped forward to hear his fate, his face grim under his embossed leather helmet.

"You are removed from command and banished from court," the empress raged. "You will not show your face to me again in this lifetime, nor will any of your family."

"As you command, Most Revered One."

Jao stalked toward her litter, turned and addressed Max. "I shall not forget your bravery, Lord Bro-dai. You will be suitably rewarded."

"I want no reward, Majesty."

"Nevertheless, you shall have it."

The mood during the return trip to the city was somber and grim. Max rode beside Cassie, torn between relief that he'd shoved both her and the empress out of harm's way, and sympathy for the hapless archer and his officers.

As they approached the city, a bolt of lightning forked out of the clouds piling up in the sky to the south. Only then did he remember Cassie's prediction.

"Please tell me those clouds are coming this way," he muttered.

"They're coming this way."

Chapter 8

*Before you embark on a journey of
revenge, dig two graves.*

—Confucius

Word of the empress's near miss raced
like a prairie fire and preceded the processional into the city. The gongs announcing
her return sounded like death knells. The
streets were almost empty as nervous resi-

dents shut themselves behind locked doors in fear of retribution.

By the time Cassie and Max reached their quarters, the palace was buzzing with whispers of a foiled assassination plot, of a planned revolt led by the empress's oldest son, of gods angered by some slight or another.

"That was some exhibition," Cassie muttered when she and Max gained the privacy of their rooms. "The Dragon Lady doesn't make much allowance for human error."

"If it was error."

"What? You think those assassination rumors are true?"

"I think they could be." Shrugging, Max removed the wolf pelt. "Jao is a woman wielding power in a man's world. Die-hard Confucianists think that's a very unnatural state of affairs."

"Ha! Not just Confucianists. Those diehards come in every shape, size and century."

Max nodded, but her comment about the empress allowing little margin for human error reminded him again of the forecast for rain. If the skies didn't open soon, Max might have to demand Cassie's life as his promised reward.

Too wound up by the morning's events, he paced their rooms until Peony led in a troop of servants with the midday meal. Max wasn't hungry, but his jump partner wielded her chopsticks with increasing skill through a parade of dishes that included pheasant in brown bean sauce, steamed lotus root, Mongolian braised pork and noodles washed down with sips of fragrant tea.

Peony took Max's lack of appetite as a personal failure. Distressed, she pleaded with him in her soft voice. "I hear from the other servants that master covered himself with great honor today. Please to tell me which foods you wish prepared and I will obtain them from the empress's own cooks."

"How about a burger and a Bud light?" he muttered, still coiled tight.

The maid's brow furrowed. "I have rosebud tea but it is dark green, not light. This bur-ger I do not know."

"It's a special dish from our land," Cassie explained with a speaking look at Max. "Beef, ground up and shaped like a pancake, then grilled and served on bread."

"Ah, so!" The maid's face cleared. "In my land, we raise the finest of Kobe beef. It is bred according to strict tradition and fed on wheat and sake, with daily massages to soften the muscle. The beef here in China is not as tender, but I shall have it ground and make a pancake of it, as you suggest."

When she gathered the empty bowls and left, Cassie shook her head. "Way to go, Brody. Nothing like messing with history."

"Don't worry. We both know the idea won't catch on for another thirteen or fourteen centuries." He glanced at the oiled rice paper covering the windows. "Where the hell is that rain you predicted?"

"It's coming. Soon."

He pushed away from the table and went into the walled courtyard. Cassie joined him a short time later, his wolf pelt draped over her shoulders, and sniffed the air.

"Can't you smell it?"

All Max could smell was the heavy scent of spicy Mongolian pork. Frowning, he scanned the small square of sky visible above the walls. It was darker than before, almost gunmetal-gray, but so far hadn't produced any moisture.

"Listen!" Cassie cocked her chin. "Hear that rumble?"

He tilted his head, straining to hear what she had, and got hit in the eye. Grunting, he knuckled his lid. "I hope that wasn't a bird flying by."

"It wasn't," she said gleefully. "Brace yourself. Here it comes."

The first few splats raised little waterspouts in the ornamental pond. Several more pattered onto the stone temple housing the goddess Guan Yiu. Then the heavens opened and the rain bulleted down. Riding a wave of relief, Max whipped an arm around Cassie's waist and swung her in a circle.

"You did it, Spring Leaf!"

She turned her face up to his. Her wet, spiked lashes framed laughing green eyes. "Not me, Brody the Barbarian. Mother Nature."

Max didn't intend what happened next. He didn't even know it was coming. Later, much later, he would tell himself it was a combination of relief and exultation that made him swoop in for a celebratory kiss.

But there was only one explanation for the jolt that hit him when his mouth locked on hers. Lust, pure and simple. The scent of her, the taste of her rain-wet lips, ignited an instant heat in his belly.

After a moment of stiff surprise, her mouth opened under his. Max didn't stop to think, didn't so much as consider the consequences of his rash act. Widening his stance, he tightened the arm banding her waist and speared his other hand through her wet hair.

The shaggy wolfskin slid off her shoulders. Her arms came up to lock behind his neck. They stood hip to hip, mouth to mouth, the cold rain sheeting down around them. Max could feel her body straining against his, feel his own hardening in response.

The iron grip he'd kept on himself the past two nights disintegrated. The grim realities of their mission got shoved to the edges of his mind. He wanted this woman with an urgency that ate into him like nothing had before.

"Master!"

Max jerked his head up and smothered a curse when he spotted Peony darting toward them. Rain soaked her gown as she dodged puddles and rushed up to them.

"Chief Eunuch Tai has come with a message from the empress," the maid gasped, gesturing toward the figure who stood in the open doorway, his arms folded across his chest and his jaw tight.

If looks could kill...

Cassie was right, Max thought. He'd made an enemy there. What he couldn't understand, though, was the hot greed that came into the eunuch's eyes when they raked over

Cassie's drenched robes. The man had been castrated, for God's sake!

Then again, look what she did to Max himself. One kiss had damn near doubled him over.

He met her eyes and saw his own frustration mirrored in their green depths. The fact that she'd felt the same hot desire provided scant consolation as he scooped up the wolf pelt, draped it over her now-shivering form and steered her toward the waiting Tai.

Once inside, Max shook off the rain and addressed the eunuch. "What's the message?"

"Her Most Heavenly Empress commands you to appear in the north hall at the hour of the tiger, when she will invest you with the rank of duke."

The eunuch delivered the message without inflection, but he wasn't happy about it. That was apparent when he turned to Cassie.

"You are ordered to consult with the imperial astrologer this afternoon. Together, you and Lord Sing will study the omens and recommend the most propitious time and date to begin the celebrations for the Fourfold Assembly of the Twelve Thousand."

Max heard Cassie's swift, indrawn breath even as his own pulse skipped a couple beats. This was it! The big show! If modern-day historians were correct, Jao would take advantage of this Buddhist holy day to step out from behind the shadow of her ailing husband and take the reins of government firmly in her own hands.

The festivities culminating in the Fourfold Assembly of the Twelve Thousand—the day Buddha's thousands of disciples spontaneously gathered from the four corners of the world—traditionally took place in March. But there was no accurate record of the exact day the great fete began in AD 674. None that Professor Carswell had been able to find, anyway. Some texts placed it on the third day following the full moon, some the day before.

Everything depended on the mercurial

March weather. Sunshine would symbolize the gods' approval of the ceremonies and, by extension, of Jao's authority. Storms or snow could be interpreted as a bad omen and cause heads to roll. A now-familiar tension kinked Max's gut as Tai stabbed a finger toward Peony.

"You! Assist Spring Leaf to change, and dress her hair. I am to escort her to the chambers of the imperial astrologer at once."

"You'll escort us both," Max countered.

His thoughts whirling, he dried off with the towel Peony hastily provided while the maid herself scurried into the sleeping chamber with Cassie.

Did this command mean the "seer" was still being tested? Or had the rain this afternoon convinced the empress to accept the gift from her duke-to-be? Either way, Max wasn't letting Cassie get swallowed up and lost from sight in this vast palace.

Excitement crawled along Cassie's nerves like fire ants as she and Max trailed Tai through a series of richly decorated corridors.

She'd spent a childhood marked by extraordinary sensitivity to nature's vagaries. In college, she'd majored in meteorology and took a minor in biology to better understand natural phenomena. As an air force weather officer, she had been trained to support air and ground assaults using data from the global to the mesoscale. Her analyses had incorporated real-time observations, upper-air soundings, National Aviation Weather Processor model visualizations, lightning analysis and weather radar reflectivity products. She'd also been one of the first air force officers trained on the updated Global Assimilation of Ionospheric Measurement model.

Cassie fully appreciated modern technology, but her own inbred instincts engendered a healthy respect for the knowledge acquired by the ancients over past millennia. The prospect of actually sitting down with an astrologer who had access to more than a thousand years' worth of accumulated knowledge both excited her and scared the dickens out of her.

But neither emotion came anywhere close to the kick in the gut she experienced when Tai stopped in front of a red door studded with brass characters representing the twelve animals of the Chinese zodiac.

They were all there, Cassie noted. The dog, the rat, the snake, the rabbit. Then her glance shifted to the symbols embedded into timbers framing the door, and the air squeezed out of her lungs.

Those symbols were constellations! Sagittarius. Capricorn. Virgo. And there, across the upper beam, was the star cluster of the Pleiades!

Her heart thudding, Cassie recognized the shapes depicted on the medallion pieces brought back by other Time Raiders—Delia Sebastian, Tessa Marconi and Alex Patton. These were painted on wood, not carved in bronze. But they were the first indication that those constellations held special significance here at the court.

While Tai rapped importantly on the door, she poked Max with a sharp elbow and jerked her chin toward the symbols. She saw him glance up, felt him tense. A frisson of excitement passed between them, quickly suppressed when the door was opened by a middle-aged man in the long blue robe and black button hat of a scholar.

"Chief Eunuch Tai has brought Lord Brodai and the seer, Spring Leaf, to see Imperial Astrologer Sing."

The scholar bowed politely to Cassie. "The master awaits you. Please come with me."

With a final glance at the symbols, she followed their escort into a small antechamber. He signaled Tai to wait there, then lifted a leather curtain and ushered her and Max inside another chamber.

She wasn't sure what she expected. Witches' kettles emitting curls of steam, maybe, or stacks of diviners' rods propped against the walls. A giant tortoise shell for deciphering the omens in its patterns. At the very least, a black-painted ceiling studded with the signs of the zodiac done in diamonds and pearls.

Instead she and Max entered a large, airy chamber warmed by braziers. Patterned wool rugs and wall coverings suppressed the drafts. Rich furs covered the benches arranged around the master's chair.

Twelve men occupied the benches, all wearing the blue gown of scholars and small round hats to cover their topknots. When they turned to stare at Cassie, she saw each also wore a gold pendant depicting a different animal of the zodiac. Experts, she guessed, steeped in the knowledge of their particular sign. And all extremely suspicious of this interloper in their midst. She felt a dozen pairs of eyes stabbing into her back as she bowed to their master.

"This priestess from a distant land is humbled and honored to be invited to consult with Her Majesty's most learned imperial astrologer."

Lord Sing sat in the high-backed chair, stroking his beard. Both he and Cassie knew she was here by royal command, not invitation, but he accepted her deferential greeting with a nod that set the ruby button on his hat winking.

"I look forward to working with you, priestess."

"And I you, most revered one."

He invited Max to take a seat on one of the benches, and gestured Cassie to a spot beside his chair.

"Will you take tea and sesame cakes?"

"Yes, thank you."

His rheumy eyes studied her while servants brought the refreshments. "When you have drunk your tea, priestess, perhaps you will tell me what omens you used to divine rain this afternoon?"

"I will most gladly, Lord Sing. In turn, I hope you will teach me the signs you used."

"You are too young to learn them. That knowledge can only come to you with another forty or fifty winters. Then," he said with a chuckle, "your bones will ache as mine do when rain approaches."

Cassie responded with a ripple of laughter and the men around them relaxed a few degrees. She could still feel their suspicion, but it wasn't quite as hostile as before.

"Tell me," the astrologer said, combing his beard with those gnarled fingers, "were you born in the year of the fire dog?"

"I was indeed, learned one. How did you know?"

"It had to be either that or the year of the earth tiger. You have been taken from your land and sold into slavery, yet nothing can quench your fire or your power."

His gaze dropped to the silver cuff banding her arm, then drifted to the identical one on Max's wrist. When it returned to Cassie, a smile appeared briefly under his drooping white mustaches.

"Does Lord Bro-dai control you, or you him?"

"Perhaps there is some of both, most learned one."

"Ah, yes. It is always so with those whose destinies are entwined for all time."

All time? Cassie fought to contain her start of surprise. Had the astrologer penetrated their disguises? Did he suspect they were from a time far in the future? Or did he see something she didn't?

As he sipped his tea, she sneaked a glance at Max. She hadn't really thought beyond their mission. What would happen when they returned to their own century? Would Max rejoin his unit? Would she ever see him again?

Probably not. They didn't have anything in common except their search for the medallion. Once they got back to their own time— *if* they got back—they would each go their separate ways.

The realization produced a surprisingly hollow feeling in the pit of Cassie's stomach. Gulping, she tried to rationalize it away. They'd been through so much these past few days, shared such close quarters. Naturally she would feel a bond.

Then there was that kiss a while ago....

Her stomach hollowed again, so tight and fast she had to wrench her attention back to the imperial astrologer.

"When you finish your tea," he said calmly, "we will consult the omens to determine the best day to begin the ceremonies of the Fourfold Assembly of the Twelve Thousand."

"I'm most eager to do so, Master Sing. And if we have time, will you tell me about the symbols on the lintel above the door to your chambers?"

"The constellations? What is your interest in them?"

"I'm interested in all things, learned one, but the stars have great significance in my land." She hesitated a moment, weighed the risks of showing her hand and took the plunge. "Legend has it that such signs were once inscribed in a bronze disk of great antiquity. Have you heard of such a disk, or seen pieces of it?"

"Perhaps."

Her excitement returned with a wild rush. At last! Their first indication that the piece of the medallion they'd come to find might actually be somewhere in the vicinity. Struggling to conceal her leaping emotions behind a placid expression, Cassie made a polite request. "Will you tell me of it?"

"Perhaps," he said again, slanting her a sideways glance. "We will speak of it after the Fourfold Assembly of the Twelve Thousand. For now, we must devote all our attention to ensuring the days and times we recommend to the empress for the ceremonies are most propitious, must we not?"

"We must indeed."

"The sly old dog!"

The emotions Cassie had struggled to contain burst their bounds the moment she and Max returned to their chambers to prepare for his anointment as a duke of the realm.

"He knows where the piece of the medallion is! I know he does."

"Then we'd better hope the sun shines on the day you two chose for the start of the festivities," Max said with some feeling, "or the knowledge might die with him."

"Thanks a lot. Make me feel good about our prediction, why don't you?"

Sheer nerves tempered her excitement. After a grueling four hours of combining their knowledge and best guesses, Cassie and Lord Sing had decided on the day before the full moon for the start of the great fete. Sing would present their recommendation to the empress when he delivered her star chart for the week.

That gave Jao five days to summon her nobles to the capital. Five days for the palace cooks to prepare a great feast. Five days for Cassie and Max to wait until—hopefully!— the astrologer clued them in to the location of the bronze medallion piece.

Five days, and four nights with Max.

The thought did funny things to her stomach again. Thoroughly disgusted, Cassie summoned Peony to help rig her out in her finest robes.

"Do me up right," she told the little maid. "I gotta go watch Bro-dai the Barbarian become a duke."

Chapter 9

*Life is really simple but men insist on
making it complicated.*

—Confucius

Bev Ashton stalked down the corridor leading
to Athena Carswell's office. The marine in her
sounded in every rifle-sharp crack of her heels
on the tiles. With each step, she swatted the
thin report clutched in her right hand against
the leg of her charcoal-gray pantsuit.

"We've got a problem," she announced grimly as she swept into Athena's office.

The professor's eyes flooded with instant alarm. "Cassie and Max? They signaled? They need immediate extraction?"

Her white lab coat flapping, Athena leaped out of her chair. Bev halted her headlong rush toward the transport area with a quick negative. "No, they haven't signaled."

Relief coursed over Athena's heart-shaped face. Blowing out a shaky breath, she put a hand to the brown hair that was always threatening to spill free of its careless twist.

"Then what's the problem?"

"Not what," Bev said, her jaw tight. "Who. Specifically, my neighbor Allen Parker. Or whoever is purporting to be Allen Parker."

"I don't understand."

Bev held up the report clenched in her fist. "I had our computer whizzes run an inquiry on Parker. According to his financials, he used his American Express card to purchase a flight to D.C. and tickets to a performance at the Kennedy Center on Tuesday night. He also had room reservations at the Willard, and a homebound flight scheduled for today. None of which he canceled when he decided to stay here in Flagstaff and cook dinner for me instead."

Athena blinked in surprise. "You had dinner with him? Isn't this the neighbor you said would never pass the military's 'don't ask, don't tell' test?"

"That's another thing." To her disgust, Bev felt a surge of heat rise in her cheeks. "At dinner… We…well, sort of clicked."

The professor was too polite to let her jaw drop, but couldn't hide her astonishment. "You and Mr. Pinkie?"

"Exactly." Frowning, Bev hitched a hip on her partner's desk. "Parker acted as swishy as usual at first, but by the end of the evening he'd transitioned. Or maybe the right word is *transformed*. In any case, he was starting to look *very* good to me. Then, when I got ready to leave, he nuzzled my neck and messed around in my head somehow. I damn near had an orgasm on the spot."

The memory of the cataclysmic sensations that had short-circuited her entire system tightened Bev's mouth into a grim line.

"I think he's a Centaurian, Athena. Either he always was and is just now showing his hand, or he's taken over Parker's body. My guess is he hopes to use me to access the lab and/or the pieces of the medallion we've recovered."

The professor chewed on her lower lip. Centaurians weren't the only ones out to sabotage Project Anasazi and steal the medallion sections. The private investigators Bev hired after the break-in at Athena's house had tracked the burglars to a corporation with so many impenetrable layers and double blinds they still couldn't ID the person or persons behind it. Given the vast sums of money involved, though, whoever it was had to have a corner on the petroleum or pharmaceutical or video-game market.

"How do you propose we handle this pseudo neighbor?" Athena asked.

Her unquestioning support eased a little of

the tension that had Bev by the throat. Despite their differences, she and the professor made a heck of a team.

Athena Carswell was soft-spoken and so brilliant it made Bev's head hurt just to try to keep up with her. By contrast, the Marine Corps had honed Bev's leadership skills and toughened her in ways the professor couldn't begin to comprehend. Together, she and Athena would take Allen Parker—or whoever he was—apart.

"Okay, here's my thinking," Bev said. "You possess the starship navigator gene. Using the crown, you can transport people through time and space. So maybe, just maybe, you could do to Parker what he did to me."

Athena's eyes widened. "You want me to mess around inside his head and give him an orgasm?"

"I'll leave that part up to you. Mostly, we need to blunt whatever power he possesses."

"I'll do it." Her mouth set in a determined line. "If your neighbor is in fact susceptible to sine waves, he's in for the ride of his life."

"Attagirl!" Bev high-fived her and pushed off the corner of the desk. "We'd better wait until we retrieve Cassie and Max, though."

"Most definitely! If I engage in a mind battle with someone who possesses the same powers I do, it could affect my ability to bring them back. I will *not* lose any more Time Raiders."

"I'll stall him," Bev promised. "Let's just hope we get a signal from Cassie and Max soon."

Real soon.

To Cassie's surprise, the days before the Fourfold Gathering of the Twelve Thousand whizzed by in a blur of frenetic activity.

Most of that was due to Max's new status at court. The empress not only granted him the title of duke, she invested him with the lands and revenues of the general she'd banished. Suddenly fabulously wealthy, he became an overnight favorite among courtiers anxious to curry favor. Invitations poured in to dinners, to theatrical performances, to wrestling matches and poetry readings.

Cassie was almost as popular. Everyone wanted a glimpse of the seer or, better yet, her input on their star charts. She made several visits to the Court of the Blue Hyacinth to consult with the emperor's concubines, all but abandoned now that Jao ruled in her enfeebled husband's name. The imperial exchequer requested her opinion on when the sap would rise in the mulberry trees so he could calculate the silk-worm tax for the coming year. Even Inspector Li came to let Cassie know he expected a suitable reward for bringing her and Max to the attention of the empress.

As busy as the days were, the nights were pure hell. Cassie lay beside Max, listening to his breathing, remembering their kiss, aching to touch him. She managed to restrain herself, however, until the night before the festival was scheduled to commence.

Max had attended another banquet, this one with Jao present. Cassie could smell the empress's distinctive lotus-and-rose perfume on him when he returned. It was late, past midnight, and tension over tomorrow's weather had Cassie wound up tight.

"Well?" she demanded when he dismissed Peony and the other servants, insisting he could undress himself. "How many heads did Her Heavenly Majesty order whacked off tonight?"

Shrugging, he dropped his boots to the floor. "None that I know of."

"Can it be? Is the Dragon Lady getting soft in her old age?"

"C'mon, Cassie. You know Wu Jao is no more cruel or despotic than any male ruler of her time, in China or anywhere else in the world." He let his other boot drop to the floor. "You also know the nobles will rise up against her at the first sign of weakness. That's why the ceremony tomorrow is so important."

As if Cassie needed the reminder! Lips pursed, she watched while Max shrugged out of the burnished-leather jacket and gold-embroidered tunic his new rank entitled him to wear. When he pulled the tunic over his head, she became so absorbed in the sight of his rippling biceps she only half heard his next comment.

"The woman is holding an empire together with skill, cunning and an iron fist, yet she's lost none of her femininity. It's easy to see why two emperors fell for her, and fell hard."

The bit about femininity caught Cassie's attention. The falling-hard part angled her chin.

"Two emperors and one twenty-first-century civil engineer?" she asked sweetly.

Too sweetly, dammit! She could have kicked herself when amusement glinted in Max's gray eyes.

"Jealous, Spring Leaf?"

"Not hardly," she lied. "The only thing going on between you and me, Brody, is our mission."

"Oh, yeah? What about that kiss in the garden?"

So it had been preying on his mind, too! Cassie couldn't decide whether she was gratified or just relieved to know she wasn't the only one. Still, she tried to keep the matter in perspective.

"We both know the kiss didn't mean anything. We were excited because of the rain and, uh, got a little carried away."

"That so?"

His gaze dropped to her mouth. The lazy amusement in his eyes edged into something different, something that made Cassie's toes curl.

"What's our excuse this time?" he asked.

She was right, Max assured himself. A kiss was just a kiss. In this instance, a small, insignificant release of nervous tension before the ceremony that would culminate in Jao's declaration that she would rule all China in place of her incapacitated husband.

Max was prepared this time, sure he could control his hunger. God knew he'd kept it on a tight leash this past week. He was thinking of those agonizing hours with Cassie lying beside him when his mouth brushed hers.

He would have stopped there. He was sure

of it. Pretty sure, anyway. If she hadn't made that small sound. Or laid her palms on his chest. Or looked up at him with such a dangerous mix of doubt and desire.

"We shouldn't do this."

"You're right," he acknowledged as he bent to brush her mouth again.

"This is crazy," she whispered, her lips pliant under his. "Stupid."

"Agreed."

He slid a hand to her nape. His conscious mind registered the textures of warm skin and soft, feathery curls, but his body reacted instinctively. Just the feel of her, the scent of her, got him hard.

Max knew then he was in trouble. Big trouble. She was like a shot of some high-powered drug that went straight to his veins. There were some questions in the back of his mind she hadn't answered yet. He still wanted to know what had really happened the day Jerry Holland died. But at this moment Max wanted Cassie more.

He'd gotten to know all aspects of her

during this mission. Her courage and gritty determination. Her kindness to the little maid. Her psychic instincts about the environment around her. Those qualities stirred his admiration almost as much as her long legs and slender curves fed his hunger.

Still, Max would have ended it after the second kiss. He came within a breath of stomping across the courtyard to the bathhouse and dousing himself with icy water. But when he dragged his head up, one look at her face told him that she wanted him as much as he did her.

He saw it in the flush staining her cheeks, heard it in the catch in her breath. That little gasp acted on Max like a spur. He tugged her closer until she lay half across his lap, and speared his fingers through her hair, anchoring her head in his palm.

"If we don't stop now," he warned hoarsely, "we don't stop."

The doubt was still there in her eyes, battling with desire, until she blew out a ragged breath and gave up the fight.

"So don't stop."

That was all Max needed to hear. His blood rushing south, he covered her mouth with his.

Cassie closed her eyes and ignored the warning shriek inside her head. She knew surrendering to this burning heat wasn't only stupid, it was downright dangerous. She and Max were in a foreign culture and a different century. One slip and they could irrevocably jeopardize their mission. One mistake and they might never find the fourth medallion piece. Hadn't she learned her lesson with Jerry Holland, for God's sake?

She had only one excuse for this monumental idiocy. Max wasn't Jerry. He wasn't anything *like* cocky, full-of-himself Jerry Holland.

Okay, maybe two excuses. They were alone, with the palace settling in for the night and the prospect of Cassie's move to different quarters looming closer with each whir of the water clock.

Not to mention the fact that Max's mouth

and hands were doing things to her central nervous system that had never been done before!

She could feel the nerves just under her skin jumping everywhere he touched. Her bare arm, when he rubbed his hand down it. Her nipples, when his fingers skimmed over the thin silk covering her breast. Her hip, when his palm slid over its curve to cradle her bottom. Then he stretched her out on the sleeping platform and Cassie stopped thinking about anything but the hunger that had grabbed her by the throat.

She dragged him down with her, their arms and legs tangled, their mouths still fused. His weight crushed her into the furs. His bare chest and shoulders provided fertile field for exploration, first with greedy hands, then with her tongue and teeth.

When she twisted to get at the buckle of his leather belt, she tore the fragile silk of her nightdress. One shoulder dragged down, baring her to the waist.

Max's growl when he bent to nuzzle her

breast kicked in her afterburner. The rasp of his tongue on her turgid nipple almost put her in orbit. Gasping, she yanked on his belt.

"We need…to…get you out of these… pants."

He took care of that with a few quick moves, and bunched a fist in the folds of the torn silk. What remained of her nightdress joined the heap of his boots, trousers and tunic.

Cassie didn't have time to generate even a momentary embarrassment over her naked-ness. She was too busy gulping at the sight of Max's. She knew the man was built. She'd seen him in the buff, or close enough to it, and had cradled against him for warmth more than once.

But this was the first time she got a full frontal. Her greedy gaze drank in the broad shoulders, the solid chest and flat stomach with its interesting tan line. Below that, he sported an erection that made her vaginal muscles spasm. It jutted from the golden hair at his groin, as stiff and as proud as the pikes carried by the imperial guards at the…

"Oh, no! We can't do this."

Cassie's groan stopped Max half on, half off the bed. She dragged her gaze upward to quivering biceps, a corded throat and a suddenly tight jaw.

"Second thoughts?" he growled.

"No! Yes! I mean…" She sat up and pounded the bunched furs in frustration. "I don't know about you, but I didn't pack any condoms for this little jaunt through time. And don't even *suggest* oiled rice paper or a sheath cut from a pig's bladder."

"Is that what they use?"

"Along with some rather nasty implements I refuse to insert into any of my orifices."

"Not a problem. We'll improvise."

When he gripped her ankle, she caught a flash of his silver cuff, a mere glimpse of cloudy quartz, before he gave her a quick tug. A second later she was flat on her back. With a wicked grin, Max reached for her other ankle. Dragging her legs apart, he made himself comfortable between her thighs. Then he contorted his torso and found her hot, wet center with his tongue.

Cassie's head went back. Her fists dug into the furs. For a fleeting second she wished she'd let Peony shave down there. Especially when Max slid a finger inside her. Two fingers. A third brushed tantalizingly close to her butt crack.

She squeezed her eyes shut and gave herself up to the erotic sensations. The prickle of his whiskers against her inner thighs. His tongue flicking her nub. His busy, busy fingers. All too soon the pleasure swirling low in her belly gathered speed and intensity. It came in waves, each more powerful than the last, until her back arched and her womb contracted, hard and tight.

"Max," she gasped, trying to wiggle back and slow things down. "It's… It's too soon, too quick! You need to… Oooh!"

The groan ripped from Cassie's throat. Head tipped back, her body torqued, she rode the explosive climax to its last, racking shudder.

"As they say here in seventh-century China," she said with a ragged breath, "holy moley!"

A deep chuckle brought her eyelids fluttering up. Max was propped on one elbow, looking extremely smug.

For an instant, just an instant, his self-satisfied grin reminded her of Jerry Holland's humiliating triumph after getting into the weirdo weather officer's pants.

As quickly as the thought came, Cassie stomped it into the dust. She knew with everything that was female in her this time was different. *Max* was different. With the gut certainty, a section of the Great Wall she'd erected around her heart cracked and came tumbling down.

"Is that what they say?" he asked with a smile that crinkled the skin at the corners of his eyes.

Another section of the wall came down. Cassie had to fight for breath.

"It…it sounds better in Chinese."

She lifted a hand, let it trail over his

shoulder, while the last ripples subsided and strength flowed back into her limp body.

"I seem to recall another ancient saying," she said, letting her hand slide over his chest and down his belly. "Something about there being many paths to the top of the mountain."

She closed her hand around his still rigid erection. The skin was satin smooth, the veins hot and pulsing. Her own sluggish pulse stirred in response. Throwing off her sensual lethargy, Cassie ran her tongue over her lips and smiled provocatively.

"My turn to take you to the mountaintop, Bro-dai."

Peony knelt on the other side of the wall separating the sleeping chamber from the gathering room. With her stockinged feet folded under her, she leaned forward to peer through the viewing hole. It was invisible from the other room, buried as it was amid the clouds and swirls in an elaborately painted wall hanging.

She'd been watching for some time. While she admired Lord Bro-dai's well-sculpted body, she thought he'd brought the mistress to the first of her prescribed seven consistencies rather too quickly. Now Spring Leaf serviced him. Interesting that they chose to swallow each other's essence instead of performing some variation of the dragon dance. Did the master not wish her to present him with a male child? If so, Peony would have to procure mercury and ground ivory for the medicinal soup used by courtesans and prostitutes to flush out the male seed after copulation.

But first she would have to inform Chief Eunuch Tai that the outlanders had, indeed, engaged in sexual congress. The prospect made Peony sick with dread. She didn't understand the eunuch's obsession with knowing every detail about the mistress's day- and nighttime activities. Or his perverted desire for a woman who could never bring him to pleasure.

Yet he seemed to want her all for himself.

The fact that she'd slept next to Lord Bro-dai these past nights ate into him like water dripping relentlessly on stone.

Tai would beat Peony for bringing this news. She knew it. She dared not withhold it, though. He would have her head if he found out about this session from one of the other servants, or overheard the master and mistress speak of it. Swallowing a sigh, Peony shifted silently on her folded knees and put her eye to the peephole once again.

Chapter 10

Be not ashamed of mistakes and thus make them crimes.

—Confucius

Startled out of sleep, Cassie shot upright in bed.

"What was that?"

The silk-lined bed furs slithered down her naked body and puddled in her lap. She blinked owlishly in the hazy dawn light, trying to figure out what had penetrated her stupor.

She thought at first it was subconscious worry about the weather on the empress's big day. The light seeping through the oiled rice paper reassured her somewhat on that point. The sun was on its way up.

So why had she jerked awake?

She was still trying to figure it out when Max rolled over and squinted at her through a half-open eye. "What was what?"

"If I knew, I wouldn't be asking."

He opened his other eye and hiked a brow at her terse reply, but didn't comment as he angled up beside her. Side by side they listened to the muted sounds of the palace getting ready for the great Buddhist festival of the Fourfold Gathering of the Twelve Thousand.

A cock crowed somewhere outside the walls. The faint clack of wooden clogs on the cobbled outer courtyard drifted through the rice paper covering the windows, along with the scent of fresh-cooked noodles. After a moment or two Cassie picked up the clink of spears and the measured stamp of booted feet.

The changing of the imperial guards. Their steady tread should have reassured her. If something was wrong, they would be hotfooting it to the scene.

Yet the hair on the back of her neck still tingled. Straining every sense, she stared at the covered windows for some clue why.

"It's the big day," Max said quietly after several moments. "Could be nerves."

"Quiet, please."

He complied and didn't say anything more until she finally gave up and rolled out of bed.

"You always this grumpy after a wild night of sex?" he asked as she reached for her torn nightdress. "I'm not complaining, you understand. I'd just like to know for future reference."

The future-reference bit caught Cassie's attention. She held the thin silk to her front while the chill dawn air mass-produced goose bumps on her rear.

"Look, Max, about last night…"

"Yeah?"

"It was good. Okay, great," she amended reluctantly. "But really, really stupid. We both knew that going in."

Poor choice of words, she realized instantly. They'd been in, out and all over each other for most of the night. The memory of some of those erotic insertions made her face heat and tipped one corner of Max's mouth into a salacious grin.

"We'll talk about it at breakfast," she said, slithering into the remnants of her nightdress. "I've got to hit the bathing room."

No way she was using the chamberpot with him lying there watching her like some Oriental potentate.

She grabbed one of the furs to use as a wrap and shoved her feet into the wooden clogs kept ready beside the door. Peony and the other servants had obviously been up for some time. Curls of steam rose from the stones in the bathhouse. Fragrant soaps and twigs for scraping teeth were laid in readiness.

Peony herself shuffled in as Cassie finished scrubbing her face and teeth. The maid looked tired this morning. No wonder, considering the hours she and the others had to serve. The loops and coils of her glossy black hair lacked some of their usual precision and the flaps of her peach-colored kimono were crooked, but she smiled as she held out arms laden with gleaming silks and thick furs.

"Chief Eunuch Tai begs you to accept these garments to wear for this most holy of days, mistress."

When she spread the clothing on the massage table, Cassie couldn't hold back a gasp. The gown was a shimmering spring-green, richly embroidered all over in a leaf pattern with silver thread. The gown had only one sleeve, as did the sable-lined outer robe of heavy blue-green silk, also fantastically embroidered.

"I've heard rumors Princess Mei Yin's gown also has but one sleeve," Peony commented, gliding to her knees with her usual grace. "The better to draw her bow, she says.

You start new fashion, mistress. Now all women will dress like the fabled female warriors of Lo-Shun."

She leaned forward to hold up a pair of silk drawers for Cassie to step into. When she bent her head, the cowl collar of her kimono separated a little from her nape.

"Peony!" Cassie gasped. "Are those bruises on your throat?"

The maid paled, dropped the drawers and hastily adjusted her kimono. "It is nothing, mistress. Only...only shadows from dim light."

"The hell it is. Let me see."

"No!" Scuttling backward on her knees, she put out a desperate hand. "Please to not look nor touch. Humble servant not worthy of such attention."

Her obvious distress held Cassie back as the little maid scrambled to her feet.

"I will send another to assist you, mistress. Must make tea for you and master."

Cassie let her go but vowed to get to the bottom of those finger marks ringing the girl's neck. They looked as though someone had lifted her by the throat and shaken her like a rag doll.

The obvious candidate was Tai. Peony was terrified of him. But why would the eunuch hurt her? What had the maid done, or not done?

Cassie was still puzzling over the matter when she finished in the bathhouse. Dressed in her elegant new finery, she started back through the courtyard. The sun had chased away the dawn shadows, she saw with relief. Empress Wu Jao could safely proclaim the gods smiled benignly on her assumption of power.

Just as she was about to skirt the ornamental pond, Cassie stopped dead. Good God! Was that a tremor she'd just felt under her feet?

She went ramrod stiff, waiting. Listening. Straining every sense until a shiver rippled down her bare arm.

Maybe it was just the cold she'd felt. The shock of hitting the chilly morning air after the bathhouse's damp heat. She almost had herself convinced when she glanced down at the pond's surface.

Jagged cracks forked through the thin sheet of ice that had formed during the night. While Cassie watched, another crack snaked across the surface. And this time there was no mistaking the small tingle that passed through the soles of her feet.

She stood still, waiting again. Listening again. Scarcely daring to breathe. Thirty seconds. A full minute. Icy sweat pooled at the base of her spine when she finally went in search of Max.

She found him in the sitting room, chowing down on a breakfast of congee—a watery rice gruel flavored with chicken and pork—and deep-fried dough sticks that tasted much like French crullers.

"Did you just feel anything?" she asked him.

He paused with a dough stick halfway to his mouth. "Like what?"

"The floor shuddering under you? A tremor in the earth?"

"No to both." His chopsticks came down. "Did you?"

She nodded. "I think so. Out there in the garden. And earlier this morning. That could have been what woke me up. If I didn't know better, I'd say the plates under this corner of the earth are preparing for a major shift."

"*Do* you know better?"

"Yeah, well, that's the sixty-four-thousand-dollar question."

Her mind churning with doubt, Cassie dropped onto the cushion beside his.

"I spent weeks researching meteorological and topographical data in preparation for this jump. Professor Carswell put her whole team at the lab on it, too. Nowhere in that exhaustive research did we find a record of any significant seismic activity during this century."

"So what makes you think there was? Or will be?"

"I felt it. I'm sure I did. And the ice in the pond cracked."

"How soon?"

Cassie wavered, consumed by uncertainty and self-doubt.

Just like last time.

No! This was worse than last time. Jerry Holland had clouded her senses. Max completely overwhelmed them. He was in her head, in a way Jerry never had been. And in her heart, dammit! She'd yielded more than her pride last night.

Suddenly, urgently frightened for him, she laid her hand over his and gripped it hard. "I don't know *when* it's coming. It could be today. It could be tomorrow or next week. Whenever it hits, my gut says we won't get much warning. I think… I think you should activate your ESC and return to our century."

"Right. I'll just beam myself home and leave you here, searching for the medallion piece all by your lonesome."

"You have to!"

She needed to make him understand. Had to keep him safe. She couldn't bear it if her faulty instincts cost him his life, as they had his friend.

"We both knew it was crazy to let down our guard last night, but we did it anyway. I can't let that kind of…of hunger overwhelm my senses now."

"You're right. Last night *was* crazy. We'll put the brakes on until the mission's over and we're back in our own time."

Cassie's heart leaped at that "until," but the scars from Jerry's death went too deep.

"You got your signals crossed, Brody. The sex was good. *Very* good. That doesn't mean I want you in my life, past, present or future."

"Too late," he countered with a smile. "According to the imperial astrologer our destinies are intertwined, remember?"

The awful fear that she'd screw up this mission and put him in danger reduced Cassie to begging.

"Please, Max. Please go!" Her nails gouged into his hand. "What if I miss the signals? What if I read them wrong? I can't be responsible for your death, too!"

His smile faded. The ghost of Jerry Holland hovered between them for a moment, until Max banished it.

"I was wrong to read so much into those e-mails Jerry sent me. I know you weren't responsible for his death. You couldn't be."

"Max…"

"Listen to me, Cass. I've just spent the toughest week of my life with you. We're in a different time, a different culture, yet you haven't stumbled once. I've watched you hold your own with secret police inspectors and imperial astrologers, and show nothing but kindness to little Peony. Your courage amazes me. I know in my heart there's no way in hell you caused Jerry's death."

"You're wrong!"

If it would convince him to go, she would share every sordid detail of her last, disastrous mission.

"I need to tell you what happened."

"No, you don't."

"I do! You have to understand."

She closed her eyes, feeling the steamy heat of the tropical jungle, seeing the sluggish brown river meandering by their campsite.

"Jerry was our squad leader. We were doing a forward terrain assessment. I can't tell you where. I *can* tell you we would have made it out if he hadn't waited until morning to call for an extraction. Fool that I was, I didn't realize he needed one more night in the jungle. With me."

Her voice went flat.

"He sent the other two squad members on a recon that night. Told me how much he loved me. Had me melting all over him. The next morning, I heard him bragging to one of the other squad members that he'd won the Jones bet."

She met Max's eyes, unflinching, but tortured by the memories of what had happened next.

"I demanded to know *what* bet. He tried to wiggle out of it, but finally admitted the truth. I was mortified. Hurt. Furious. Especially after he admitted my 'psycho-skills' really creeped him out."

"Jesus."

"The river must have started rising during our fight. I saw some debris sweep by. I heard what sounded like a distant rumble. My instincts started pinging, but I was too angry to listen to them. Then it roared down on us—a solid wall of brown water five feet high. We learned later that a storm had hit upriver and sent it bursting through an earthen dam."

She could still see that churning brown wall, still hear its thunder.

"The riverbank crumbled under Jerry's feet. I made a grab for him, got hold of one arm. He was too heavy and the current was too strong. The other two squad members testified that I tried to save him," she finished in a ragged whisper, "but I knew in my heart I killed him."

"The hell you did."

"I did, Max! I did! I ignored my instincts and Jerry died as a result. Now those instincts are pinging again. I've got to trust them. *You've* got to trust them."

"I do." Releasing her hand, he framed her face with both of his. "I believe in your skills, Cassandra. Implicitly. You've proved them over and over again on this mission."

"Yes, but—"

"No buts. I'm not leaving you. We landed in this century together. We'll get out of it together."

She started to protest, but Max cut her off with a swift, hard kiss. When he raised his head, she could see further argument was useless.

"Whether or not we find the medallion piece," he said fiercely, "we'll *both* activate our ESCs the moment you sense an earthquake is about to occur."

And Confucians thought women were stubborn, intractable creatures!

Dread sat like a stone in Cassie's belly, but she let out a ragged sigh and made a feeble attempt at a smile. "If that's the case, we should have departed last night, when you made the earth move. Several times."

"Which I intend to do again," he said with

a quick, slashing grin. "Once we're out of here."

He kissed her again, slower and more thoroughly, then shoved a dough stick at her.

"Eat some breakfast, woman. We've got a long day ahead of us."

Despite Max's insistence, Cassie couldn't force down more than a few spoonfuls of congee. Her nerves jumped with every sudden sound. While Max outfitted himself in the armor that befitted his new rank, she went back outside to stare at the now-melting ice in the ornamental pond.

She was wound tight as a wire when the gongs sounded to assemble for the first phase of the celebration, a procession to Chang'an's oldest and most holy temple. There the empress and her court would say prayers and make offerings to Buddha.

Tomorrow the whole entourage would ride to the tomb of the first Tang emperor, the man Wu Jao had enthralled as a junior concubine, the father of her current husband.

According to the published agenda, she would honor his spirit and those of his ancestors by burning offerings of pearls, jade, rich silks and precious scrolls.

The feasting would begin the following day—in private homes, in public gathering places and most especially at the palace. Jao would host a great banquet with all her nobles in attendance. At the culmination of the feasting, the proclamation that gave her full and absolute plenipotentiary powers would be read aloud.

The entire three days had been carefully scripted—every event, every offering. Yet Cassie couldn't shake the uneasy sense that nature might serve up an unexpected surprise.

Her antsy feeling intensified when she walked to the outer courtyard with Max. The scene was one of controlled chaos. She'd thought the processional to view the mounted drill was an incredible display of color and pageantry. It didn't compare to this one.

Every noble and lady of the court had turned out, all dressed in their glittering best. Horses with braided manes and tails stamped and tossed their heads. Chariots scraped wheels as they jostled for position. Officers shouted orders, echoed in booming voices by sergeants-at-arms, to line up troops sporting colorful banners of red and royal yellow on their tall pikes.

As a new duke, Max would ride with the nobles. Cassie should have been relegated to the ladies' clique, but had finagled a spot next to the imperial astrologer. She fully intended to hold Lord Sing to his promise to tell her about the bronze medallion he claimed to have seen.

Standing on tiptoe, she searched the ranks of mounted scholars until she spotted Sing's white beard and gleaming ruby hat button.

"There he is."

"I see him." Max signaled the attendant holding the reins of the two horses he'd purchased with his new wealth. "Let's get you in the saddle and in line."

The attendant led the animals forward. Cassie's was a sturdy chestnut bred on the fertile Three Rivers plain. Max had chosen a sleek, muscled bay for himself.

Cassie had stepped onto a marble mounting block and was just about to put her foot in the stirrup when the massive gates to the inner courtyard opened and the royal party emerged.

The empress led the entourage, accompanied by her sons, daughters and close relatives, all aligned strictly according to protocol. The entire party was resplendent in furs and shimmering silks sewn with pearls. Jao wore the Tang dynasty royal yellow trimmed in sable. Combs with cascading gold and jade ornaments adorned her hair. An attendant holding an umbrella suspended from a long pole rode behind her to protect her porcelain complexion from the sun.

She was a superb horsewoman, sitting easily on her mount. It was an Akhal-Teke, one of the golden racers bred in the far deserts and highly prized for both speed and endurance. The magnificent stallion moved with a liquid gait, head high, iron-shod hooves striking against the cobbles.

Its trappings were almost as glorious as the horse itself. The saddle cloth shimmered with gold thread. The high-pommeled saddle would be a work of art in any century. But the elaborate bridle with its fringed brow band and decorated cheek pieces sent Cassie's heart straight into her throat.

"Max!" she squeaked. "Look!"

"I am. That's one fine piece of horseflesh."

"Not the horse. Look at the bridle's brow band!"

He leaned forward, eyes narrowed against the sunlight flashing off the irregularly shaped decoration set dead center in the leather headpiece.

"That's it!" he muttered with fiercely restrained excitement. "Our piece of the Pleiadian medallion!"

Chapter 11

The cautious seldom err.

—Confucius

Cassie practically shook with excitement.
There it was! The piece of the medallion she
and Max had come to find. She was sure of
it! The bronze had been polished to a sheen
that made it glitter like gold, but the odd
shape and the markings were unmistakable.

Her heart in her throat, she followed the

empress's progress through the outer courtyard. Jao was about to move to the head of the processional when she caught sight of Cassie and Max. With a twitch of the reins, the empress brought her mount over to where they stood.

"So, Seer. You and Lord Sing chose this day well. The gods smile down on us."

"They do indeed, Most Gracious Majesty."

"If the sun continues to shine throughout the festivities, you shall be amply rewarded. What is your wish? Jewels? Lands? Your freedom?" Her gaze flicked to Max, standing at Cassie's shoulder. "Or perhaps a husband to protect and shield you?"

Whoa! That was all Cassie needed. A wedding in the seventh century before jumping back to the twenty-first.

Would it be legal? Was her destiny intertwined with Max's for all time, as the imperial astrologer had predicted? The thought popped into her head. Just as quickly, she shoved it out. This was no time for any concern but her mission.

Deciding to take full advantage of the opportunity the empress had just handed her, Cassie gestured to the decoration in the center of the brow band.

"If you would gift me with anything, Most Gracious Majesty, I would have this piece. It is most unusual."

Jao bent forward to see what she referred to and arched her delicately winged brows. "This is all you would ask of me?"

"Yes."

"It is yours. I'll have it delivered to you at the conclusion of the ceremonies."

Cassie managed not to whoop and dance on the mounting block, but it took some doing.

"I regret it's just a copy," the empress commented as she gathered her reins in her small hands. "The original was rumored to have great magical powers."

Cassie's wildly careening excitement plummeted like a dove shot through the heart by one of the imperial archers.

"This...this is a copy?"

"Indeed it is. Legend says the original was Emperor Qin's personal amulet. He carried it in every battle, mounted like this one in his warhorse's bridle. The ancients say both horse and bridle were buried in his tomb with him. I had this copy made from sketches found in an old text."

Jao's dark eyes glittered with satisfaction.

"It's fitting, is it not, that the first woman to rule all China should adopt the amulet of the emperor who created our vast empire?"

With a nod to Max, the empress flicked her reins and rejoined the royal entourage. A general scuffle ensued as the rest of the procession jostled into line and prepared to move out.

Thoroughly chagrined, Cassie used the bustle to cover her groan of dismay. "Emperor Qin? Wasn't he the one who built the Great Wall?"

"Portions of it," Max confirmed grimly. "And the terra-cotta army."

"Qin ruled, like, two hundred BC!"

The implications were staggering. They'd

missed their mark by almost a thousand years.

"Did Professor Carswell interpret the message on the third piece of the medallion wrong?" Cassie asked, her stomach sinking at the possibility. "Did she send us back to the wrong century, to confront the wrong emperor?"

A muscle ticked in the side of Max's jaw. The hand gripping their horses' reins showed white at the knuckles.

"I don't know," he replied tersely.

"And what about the tremors I felt earlier this morning?" Desperation added an edge to Cassie's voice. "Oh, God! Did we get that wrong, too? Was this part of China devastated by an earthquake before Jao took power into her own hands? Did she have all record of it expunged so history would look more favorably on her rule?"

"I don't know, dammit! But I'm—"

The boom of a massive gong drowned him out. A chorus of deep-throated horns answered. The acrobats and tumblers began to move toward the palace gates. Pennants fluttering, the advance guard fell into ranks behind them.

Max gripped Cassie's elbow with his free hand and pulled her and their horses back, out of the way.

"I'm beginning to think history may have it wrong," he said urgently. "I've been to Qin's tomb. Or at least the small portion archaeologists have excavated. The conventional wisdom is that rebels broke in and rampaged through the vast underground area housing the terra-cotta army. They smashed thousands of the clay figures and set fire to the wooden supports holding up the roof. When the supports collapsed, tons of earth crashed down, burying the army and sealing off the entrance to the rest of the tomb. But…"

Cassie gulped. "But?"

As the royal party rode by, the grip on her elbow tightened and Max's gray eyes blazed with sudden certainty.

"But I'm thinking now it could have

been an earthquake, not fire, that caused the roofs to collapse. How sure are you it's going to happen?"

All the doubts, all the crippling uncertainties, rose up and threatened to choke her. "I…uh…"

"Go with your gut, Cassie." His eyes held hers, steady, sure. "I trust your instincts."

She knew then that she'd fallen for this man, and fallen hard. Whatever happened, whatever they found or didn't find, his unquestioning belief in her healed the last ragged hole in her heart.

"It's going to happen," she said with absolute conviction. "Maybe not today or tomorrow. But soon."

"Then Professor Carswell sent us to exactly the right moment in history. We've got to get in—and out—of Qin's tomb before the earth convulses and buries the medallion, possibly for all time."

Yikes! This was alternate history with a vengeance. Cassie's stomach did another drop when she remembered her first glimpse of the high, sweeping plain north of the city. It was dotted with dozens of burial mounds. Every emperor since Qin was buried somewhere in the vicinity.

"Can you find the right tomb, Max?"

"I think so. The landmarks are all different now, but I remember taking a bead on the mountains when I drove out to the Museum of the Terra-cotta Warriors. The museum sat at fifteen degrees right of the highest peak."

Thank God for civil engineers and their fetish for precision!

Cassie flicked a quick glance at the procession, and saw that the imperial astrologer and his twelve acolytes had already passed through the gates. They were followed by the inspectors of the Bureau of Imperial Oversight and Protection of Their Most Heavenly Majesties. Cassie caught sight of Inspector Li looking their way, and ducked farther back in the shadows.

"How far off is this tomb?" she asked Max urgently.

"An hour by taxi. That makes it three,

maybe four hours on horseback." He shoved the reins into Cassie's hands. "Here, hold the horses. We'll need something to dig with and a flint to light torches once we get in."

"And bring me a pair of your pants," Cassie said urgently as he started back toward their quarters. "I can't ride in this gown."

"Will do. I'll be right back."

He dodged the tail end of the procession and disappeared. Cassie clutched their horses' reins, trying to make herself as inconspicuous as possible. At any moment she expected Inspector Li or some other harried official to ride up and demand to know why she hadn't take her place in line.

She didn't draw a full breath until Max reappeared. He wore his wolf skin over his shoulders and held a bulging drawstring sack.

"I had Peony pack us some food and a warmer cloak for you."

"And the pants?"

"And the pants. Let's go."

* * *

"Gone? Gone where!"

Peony cringed as Chief Eunuch Tai sprang out of his chair. She'd debated for more than an hour whether to inform him of Lord Bro-dai's odd request. Fear of the eunuch had finally overcome her reluctance to report on the two who had been so kind to her. That, and the knowledge that Tai would learn of their disappearance sooner or later in any case.

"I don't know where they went, master. Lord Bro-dai said only that he needed food and warm clothing for a journey. Then he snatched up his wolf pelt and left."

Fury suffused the eunuch's cheeks. In two strides he crossed the room and caught Peony by the throat.

"How much food?"

"Master!" Terrified, she beat at the hand crushing her windpipe. "Master, please!"

He lifted her off her slippered feet and shook her like a rag doll. "How much?"

"Four…dumplings," she choked out

through the searing agony. "Two cold... breasts...of hen."

So they weren't going far, Tai guessed. But where? And why?

The medallion!

His fist tightened convulsively. He paid no attention to the maid's frantic clawing as certainty burst inside him.

They'd found the medallion, or at least knew where to look for it!

Rage boiled up, consuming him. If he let the medallion slip from his grasp, Lord Kentar would be relentless. At worst, Tai would be gutted like a squealing pig and left to die. At best, he would be condemned to live forever on this accursed planet. A gelding, never to mount another mare! All because this stupid little bitch didn't come to him right away.

With a roar of pure fury, he bunched his fist, snapped her neck and threw her lifeless body against the wall.

Tai discovered moments later that he wasn't the only one searching for the outlanders.

When he went to the outer courtyard en route to the stables, he spotted a small crowd clustered near the main gates. Sobbing pleas rose from the center of the crowd, punctuated by a sharp demand.

"Which direction did they take?"

"I didn't see them, Inspector."

"Again."

There was a splash, followed by more gurgling sobs.

"Please. Please. I speak the truth."

Tai shouldered his way into the crowd. He recognized Inspector Li of Her Majesty's secret police and gave a grunt of approval when he saw the inspector was interrogating a gate guard. Two of Li's minions had the guard bent backward over a mounting block, while others stood ready with iron tongs and buckets of water.

"Hear me well," Li warned the writhing guard. "The empress was most displeased when I told her the seer and Duke Bro-dai had not joined the processional. She sent me to find out why. Now I learn they rode out shortly after we did, but no one claims to know what direction they took. They had to pass through this gate," Li said coldly, his mouth twisting into a sneer beneath his long black mustache. "You were manning the tower above the gate. You must have seen them."

"The procession..." the guard gasped tearfully. "The noise... The confusion... I don't..."

"Again."

"Aiiii!"

Ruthlessly, one of Li's subordinates forced the tongs between the man's jaws and spread them. Another upended a bucket. Gurgling and flailing helplessly, the guard choked under the torrent.

"Think hard," Li said venomously, "or your next breath will be your last. The seer was riding a chestnut, Duke Bro-dai a bay."

Tai muscled his way into the circle of torturers. "The duke might have been wearing a wolf pelt over his shoulders. Do you remember him now, guardsman?"

The inspector's fury at the interruption turned to vicious satisfaction when the guard spat out a mouthful of water and gasped.

"Yes! Yes, I saw such a pelt."

"Did the man wearing it have a woman with him?"

"Yes."

"Which way did they go?"

"They…they exited the palace gate and turned west, then north. If they left the city itself, they had to pass through the Lion's Gate."

"You'd best hope we get word of them at the Lion's Gate," Li snarled. "If we do not, I will personally stake you out here in the courtyard and drive a wooden spear through your bowels."

He turned away and strode toward his mount. When his minions leaped to follow him, Tai exerted his authority.

"You!"

He stabbed a finger at the beefiest underling. The man's horse wasn't up to Tai's weight, but he didn't have time to go to the stables for his own. He couldn't allow Li to reach Spring Leaf before he did. Lord Kentar had promised him the red-haired witch, to mount as often as he pleased…once he recovered the damned medallion.

"I will take your horse," Tai told the underling arrogantly.

"The devil you will."

"I am Chief Eunuch Tai of the Lotus Court. The empress charged me with caring for the seer. I will not let her escape."

The man looked to his boss for direction. Li met Tai's eyes, calculating, assessing.

"You think she tries to escape?"

"I do."

"Why? The empress looks on her with favor. Or did, until I informed her the seer and her keeper had not joined the processional."

Tai wasn't about to tell this sharp-nosed secret policeman about the medallion. He'd take care of Li when the time came.

"Who knows what's in the mind of outlanders?" Impatiently, he grabbed the pommel and swung into the saddle. "We're wasting time."

Cassie's certainty that disaster was only days, if not hours, away increased with every mile she and Max rode north.

The signs were subtle. Birds silent and gone to roost in the trees. A faint, acrid aroma underlying the cloying scent of the joss sticks burning in every roadside shrine and village temple. The hair that rose on the back of Cassie's neck.

Mercifully, the road was almost free of traffic. Apparently everyone was at their local pagoda observing the rituals associated with the holy day. Cassie prayed they would finish their worship before the ground began to shake and those multitiered pagodas tumbled down around them.

"Do you recognize anything?" she asked Max when they stopped at a village well to water their horses.

Jaw tight, he scanned the plain ahead. The

burial mounds seemed to stretch forever on either side. Some had elaborate temples close by so the deceased could be properly honored with offerings and prayers. Others were mere humps of earth that housed lesser mortals—wives and concubines and slaves to attend their lord in the afterlife.

Cassie racked her brain, trying to remember when the Chinese had stopped burying wives and concubines alive with their dead lord. Long before Emperor Qin, she was sure. By his time, living sacrifices had been replaced by clay figures. Hence the vast army guarding his tomb.

They were here somewhere, those thousands of silent sentinels. But where? God, what she wouldn't give for satellite infrared imaging. Or Google. Mapquest. Anything!

"We're close," Max replied.

He skimmed the distant mountain peaks, dropped his line of sight and lifted it again.

"I think… It may be…"

He sounded less decisive than Cassie had

ever heard him. She knew exactly how he felt. Shouldering her horse aside, she raised a hand to Max's cheek and gave him the same assurance he'd given her.

"Go with your gut, Brody. I trust your instincts."

"You do, huh?"

"Absolutely."

He stared down at her for long moments before scrutinizing the peaks again. Then he angled his chin toward a distant mound.

"That one."

"All right!"

She started to swing around, but he caught her arm and smiled down at her. "You're a piece of work, Spring Leaf."

She could see herself in his eyes. She saw something else, too. Something that made her soul sing before he gave her a swift, hard kiss and boosted her into the saddle.

"Remind me to tell you later that I love you," he said as he mounted his horse.

"Huh?"

He was already turning the bay into the

open field leading to the mound. Cassie scrambled to follow.

"Brody! Wait! What was that about love?"

"Later, Jones. After we figure out how to get into Emperor Qin's tomb."

The tremor hit while they were still half a mile or more from the mound. Not a major quake, Cassie sensed at once. Just a brief precursor to the one she knew would follow in the next hours or days.

But it was strong enough to make Max's mount shy and hers whinny in terror. The sturdy chestnut rose up on its rear legs, pawing the air, and Cassie tumbled from the saddle. She landed hard in an unplowed field, the wind knocked out of her. The chestnut raced off while she tried to suck air back into her lungs.

"You okay?" Max shouted as he fought to control his own skittish mount.

"Yeah."

Other than having both her dignity and her bottom bruised. Thoroughly disgusted with herself for getting thrown so easily, Cassie shoved her hair out of her eyes and pushed herself to her feet.

"Hang loose," Max instructed, "and I'll go after your... Hell! Watch out!"

The bay was as spooked as the chestnut. Humping and whinnying, it danced backward.

Cassie had to jump sideways to put some distance between herself and those lethal hooves. She landed in softer earth this time, thank goodness.

Or not!

That was her last thought before the ground crumbled beneath her feet and she dropped into a black, bottomless pit.

Chapter 12

*The man who moves a mountain begins
by carrying away small stones.*
                                    –Confucius

"Cassie!"

"I'm okay," she called up through the hole in the earth. Shaken by her fall, she blinked dirt out of her eyes and tried to pierce the gloom around her.

"I can't see much," she shouted to Max.

"It's dark as night down here. But I'm standing on some kind of a platform or something."

"Watch out. I'm coming down."

With a shower of dirt and small stones, Max dropped through the hole feetfirst and landed with a thud. Just enough light slanted through the opening for Cassie to see he'd brought the pouch with him. Moments later he'd drawn out his sword and wrapped a cloth tight around the tip. That done, he struck flint against stone until a spark leaped onto the cloth and set it ablaze.

The makeshift torch didn't penetrate the darkness much farther than the light from the hole above them. But it was enough for Max to give a long, low whistle.

"Damn! You did it, woman!"

"Did what?"

"Landed smack on top of the army guarding the entrance to Emperor Qin's tomb. Unless I miss my guess, we're standing on the roof of the pit."

"We can't be! The mound you thought

was his tomb is still half a mile or more away."

"You'll understand in a minute. Here, hold this."

With Cassie gripping the sword hilt, Max went down on one knee and used both hands to feel the uneven surface beneath them until he found an edge. A grunt and a heave later, he'd tugged up a section of what looked like corrugated tin. It was rusted and rough on the outside and painted a deep enamel blue on the inside.

"Ugh!" Cassie wrinkled her nose as stale air gushed out, but Max stuck his head through the opening. When he popped it out again, he was wearing a wide grin.

"Yep, we're here. Hand me the sword. I'll go first."

When Cassie followed him down a few moments later, her jaw dropped in sheer astonishment. She had landed between two clay archers wearing exquisitely detailed armor, right down to the decorations on their quivers. Similarly attired warriors marched in front and behind these two, their ranks stretching as far as she could see in the gloom. Each of the warriors, she saw with amazement, had different facial features and arrangements of their topknots.

She'd read about the terra-cotta warriors. Had watched video clips of them during the 2008 Beijing Olympics. But seeing them up close and personal like this, with their clothing and features still painted in the original vivid colors, sucked the air right out of her lungs.

It returned in a painful gulp when she remembered how many of these figures Emperor Qin had ordered cast from clay. An estimated eight or ten thousand, only small a portion of which had been excavated back in the twenty-first century.

And they had to find the emperor's war-horse amid this vast army before another, maybe more lethal, tremor shook the tons of earth above the blue-painted roof!

"Is this the same layout you saw during your visit?" she asked Max with a touch of desperation.

"Pretty much, except what I saw were reconstructed figures. Nothing like this."

Frowning, he swept the torch in a wide arc.

"Do you remember General Schwarzkopf's strategy during the first Iraqi war?"

Cassie blinked, surprised by the question. As a weather weenie, she would hardly qualify as a war planner, but even the most junior air force officers studied decisive engagements like Thermopylae and Waterloo and Stormin' Norman's strategy during Desert Storm.

"Sure. He called it Shock and Awe. But—Oh!"

Understanding burst like a bottle rocket. Damned if she hadn't retained more of her military training than she'd thought.

"I remember now! Schwarzkopf said in his book that he based his strategy on ancient principles."

Max gave her a quick grin. "Bingo."

Basking in his approval, Cassie dredged her memory for details. "Okay, Shock and

Awe utilized air strikes to soften the target, mechanized assault forces to open a breach and massive ground forces to control terrain and assure victory. What does that equate to in seventh-century Chinese warfare?"

"Ranks of archers launching massive volleys to soften the target," Max replied without hesitation, "followed by chariots or cavalry to crash through opposing lines, and finally, foot soldiers wielding pikes and swords."

Cassie eyed the quiver slung over the shoulder of the figure next to her. "So we're in the front ranks, with the archers?"

"Right."

"Where would the generals be positioned in relation to the rest of the troops?"

"Behind the archers, but ahead of the cavalry, so they can lead the charge."

"Would the emperor be with them?"

"Qin would. He defeated the other warlords and united all China, remember? You don't do that by relying on someone else to do your fighting for you."

Holding the makeshift torch high, Max

started down the long row between the larger-than-life-size archers. Cassie stayed right on his heels until one of the wooden poles supporting the roof gave a loud groan. The sound echoed through the vast chamber and pulled her up short.

"Max! I don't have a good feeling about this!"

He turned back immediately. "Do we need to get out?"

She stood between brightly painted warriors, listening, feeling, sniffing the musty air. She couldn't miss the subtle signs this time. She *couldn't!* Not with Max's life hanging in the balance.

"I think…I think there's time yet."

"Let's hustle."

They burst through the last ranks of archers on the run and skidded to a stop. Facing them was a seemingly endless line of mounted horsemen, each outfitted more resplendently than the last.

"Which one is Qin?" Cassie panted.

She could almost hear Max's teeth grinding in frustration. "Damned if I know. We'll have to start at the—"

"Wait!"

She grabbed his arm and thrust it upward so the flickering torch illuminated a patch of ceiling. She'd assumed it had been painted a deep blue to represent a bright, daytime sky, but this portion showed stars picked out in glittering silver.

Not just stars, but constellations!

"Look, Max. There's Capricorn." She spun in a quick circle. "And Virgo. And… Oh, God! Those are the Pleiades!"

She whipped around again, shaking with excitement.

"Wu Jao said our piece of the medallion was Qin's personal amulet. He carried it into every battle. Doesn't it stand to reason he'd have that particular constellation painted above him as he led his army into the after-life?"

Max was already on the run. Cassie had to scramble to keep up with him. She let out another whoop, this one of sheer joy, when

Max skidded to a halt in front of the statue of a magnificent warhorse in full regalia. An imperial guard stood at rigid attention, gripping its reins, as if Qin himself were going to appear at any second and leap into the saddle.

And there, embedded in the bridle's brow band, was an irregularly shaped piece of bronze. The piece of the medallion! They'd found it!

Cassie almost wept with relief. "Dig it out," she urged Max. "Quick."

Like the other figures, the warhorse was larger-than-life-size. Max's head barely came up to the muzzle. The brow strap was out of reach.

"I need something to stand on. See if—"

Both he and Cassie froze as an ominous rumble echoed through the chamber. A half second later, the ground rolled under their feet.

"Take cover!"

Max tossed the makeshift torch aside and threw himself at Cassie. They went down, his body covering hers, as clay figures started to topple.

The guard holding the warhorse's reins tipped over and cracked into a dozen pieces. The general mounted on a charger a few feet away suffered a similar fate. But when he fell, he fell sideways and hit the emperor's warhorse.

The clay horse crashed down and shattered right on top of Cassie and Max. She lay flat, squashed under Max's weight, his arms protecting her head, while more warriors toppled all around them.

Then there was silence. Utter, terrifying silence.

"Max?"

Again only silence.

"Max! Are you okay?"

Frantic, Cassie wiggled and squirmed out from under his dead weight. Professor Carswell's last warning screamed through her mind as she kicked away the broken pottery shards and struggled to tip Max onto his back.

The professor could smooth over any "debris" Cassie and Max might leave behind, so there would be no trace of their impact on historical events. But that only applied to actual historical events. If either of them was killed, not even Athena Carswell could make them whole, because they were *never really part* of that history.

Fighting blind panic, Cassie tugged Max onto his back. Nausea welled hot and acrid in her throat as she brushed the dirt from his face with shaking hands.

"Max! Max, can you hear me?"

Not again. Dear God, *please!* Not again. Jerry Holland's death had been hard enough to bear. This man she loved with every fiber of her being.

She scrabbled up onto her hands and knees, tugged back his wolf pelt and grabbed his hand. Slapping his palm over the quartz crystal set in his silver armband, she held it in place with a knee while she fumbled for her own ESC. While the quartz warmed under her palm, she chanted a furious mantra.

"You have to hear me, Max. You have to! I didn't get to tell you that I love you, too. Do you hear me, Brody? I love you."

Her crystal was getting hot to the touch when his lids fluttered up. Confusion clouded his gray eyes for a second or two before he blinked it away. He twisted his head and frowned down at his silver cuff before zinging a glance at the broken statues all around them. Enough light showed through new cracks in the earth to bring him to his feet.

"Tap the extraction code," he called to Cassie over his shoulder. "I'll get the medallion piece."

Her hand shaking, she tapped an SOS on the quartz as Max grabbed the pottery shard with the embedded bronze piece.

Then they were both up and running.

Professor Carswell had slept at the lab throughout their time jump, waiting for their signal. But once she got it, she had to don the headpiece and focus her energy before she could bring them back. That might take thirty seconds. A minute. Two. Neither Max nor Cassie wanted to wait those precious seconds in an underground tomb while the earth trembled around them.

They leaped over tumbled archers and raced back to the piece of the roof Max had pried up. With every step, Cassie could sense a major tremor coming. Praying the professor would get them out in time, she scrambled through the opening and onto the roof. Max swung up behind her a moment later and craned his neck to gauge the distance to the hole Cassie had fallen through.

"Here," he barked, linking his hands. "I'll boost you up."

Using his hands and a strong heave as a springboard, she flew upward, crawled out through the hole and flopped onto her stomach. She was stretching an arm down for Max when the earth shuddered under her belly.

"Max! Take my hand! Fast!"

He leaped up, caught her wrist and almost wrenched her arm from its socket. Cassie gritted her teeth against the agony as he used her arm as an anchor to walk up the dirt walls. Not until he was out did she realize the violent shudders under her belly were connected to the thunder behind them. She flopped over, swallowing a scream at the pain in her shoulder, and saw six horsemen charging straight at them.

Tai was in the lead, his powerful body hunched forward in the saddle and murder in his dark eyes. Inspector Li galloped at his side. His black cloak was flapping behind him like a vulture's wings.

"Oh, hell!" With a resigned sigh, Max got to his feet and reached across his waist for his sword. His mouth twisted in disgust when he remembered it was lying amid the rubble below.

Suddenly a tingle raced across Cassie's skin. The hair on her arms stood straight up. At the same instant, the ground rolled beneath her feet.

"This is it!" she shouted to Max.

He reached out, gripped her hand,

squeezed hard. Then he disappeared right before her eyes.

Cassie's last image before she, too, rode the waves, was Chief Eunuch Tai's startled face as the earth opened under his horse's hooves.

Chapter 13

*Wheresoever you go, go with all your
heart.*

—Confucius

Cassie blinked her eyes open and felt her
pulse leap with wild elation.

They'd landed back in the twenty-first
century looking exactly as they had when
they'd zoomed out of it! She was in jeans and
a fuzzy yellow sweater. Max…

She gulped, taking in his buzz-cut blond hair, thigh-hugging jeans and faded Air Force Academy sweatshirt. For a crazy instant she almost missed his wolf pelt and sexy Viking look.

Then he shook his head to clear the haze from their jump and raised his fist. In it was the pottery shard containing the embedded bronze piece.

"We did it, Jones!"

With a shout of triumph, he whipped his free hand around her waist and dragged her in for a long, hard kiss. A laughing, exultant Cassie returned it joyously.

When he raised his head, she had eyes only for him. His smile. His strong, square chin. His so very sexy and kissable mouth.

"About that unfinished conversation," he growled.

"The one on our way to Qin's tomb," she asked breathlessly, "when you said you love me?"

"I was thinking more of the one *inside* the tomb, when you said *you* love *me*."

"I didn't think you heard me!"

"I did, babe. Every word."

"Right." She put her wildly churning emotions into a radiant smile. "About that…"

"Ahem."

The discreet throat clearing echoed in Cassie's ears like a thunderclap. She jumped out of Max's arms, her face flaming as she took in the small crowd circling the glass transport capsule.

Professor Carswell was still wearing the crown-shaped headpiece she'd used to bring them back. General Ashton stood beside her. Her expression conveyed profound relief and amusement in equal proportions. Delia Sebastian had a broad smile on her face, while her jump partner, Captain Jake Tyler, gave Cassie a thumbs-up and Max a wry grin. The lab assistants and data techs were crowded around, as well, whooping and high-fiving.

Max and a thoroughly embarrassed Cassie stepped out of the capsule to a chorus of cheers. Max's first order of business was to hand Professor Carswell the broken shard. Then he turned to General Ashton and rendered a sharp salute.

"Mission accomplished, ma'am."

"Good work, you two." The general's blue eyes were warm with approval. "Judging by the vibes Athena picked up, it seemed to get hairy there at the end."

"A little," Cassie admitted with magnificent understatement.

"Well, we're all glad you're back. Things have gotten a little dicey here, too. I'll brief you after you've rested and Athena deciphers the message encoded in this piece of the medallion." She checked her watch. "Let's reconvene at fifteen hundred hours in the conference room. You can give us a full report then and we'll fill you in on what's been happening on this end."

Cassie started to protest that she didn't need rest, but Max preempted her. Looking the general straight in the eye, he nodded. "Yes, ma'am. Fifteen hundred hours."

Ashton gave him a bland smile. "That

should be enough time for you two to finish your…conversation."

"Yes, ma'am."

Cassie's cheeks were hot again when Max hustled her out of the launch facility and down a long corridor toward the crew quarters.

"We've got six hours before we reconvene," she protested. "Shouldn't we, uh, get a motel room or something?"

"Six hours isn't anywhere near enough time for what I have in mind, Jones. I don't want to waste any of it looking for a room."

Okay! That wiped out Cassie's embarrassment and sent her pulse leaping in anticipation. As eager now as he was, she stood aside so he could yank open the door to one of the crew rooms.

"Hell! This one's occupied."

"Looks like Jake's got it," Cassie muttered, eyeing the U.S. Army Special Forces sweatshirt draped over a chair.

"Yeah, it does." Max scraped a palm over his chin. "Hang loose a moment."

He disappeared into the bathroom and returned a moment later with a black shaving kit.

"Tyler won't mind," he assured Cassie as he slammed the door to that crew room and tried another. This one opened onto a room showing only neatly made twin beds and a bare bureau.

The moment Cassie stepped inside, Max tossed the shaving kit on the nearest available surface, hit the lock and backed her against the door. His arms caged her. His eyes smiled down at her.

"Now, Spring Leaf, you were saying…?"

All Cassie had to do was look up at him to know with absolute certainty. No doubts. No questions. No hesitation. Her instincts regarding this man were true and sound.

She curved a hand over his cheek. The golden bristles that had led him to appropriate a shaving kit tickled her palm as she opened her heart.

"I love you, Bro-dai the Barbarian. I don't know when it happened. Sometime after you kissed me in the rain, I think."

"I know exactly when it happened for me," he said smugly.

"You do?"

"Yep. That morning you jumped out of bed with those brown spots on your gown. Took me a while to get past that bit about ground-up antler fuzz. Once I did, though, all I could think about was what was under those spots."

He bent and brushed her mouth with his.

"I wanted you so bad I hurt with it, Cassie. Almost as much as I want you now."

He wasn't exaggerating. Obviously, he didn't need the stimulant of ground-up antler fuzz to send blood to his jade stalk. He was already rigid and hard behind the zipper of his jeans.

Cassie could feel his erection against her stomach. The muscles low in her belly tightened in response, sending erotic ripples throughout her body as she hooked her arms around his neck. Hip to hip, mouth to mouth, they released a hunger that soon consumed them.

They tore their clothes off minutes later. Or maybe it was hours. Whatever! Leaving a trail of jeans and shoes and underwear, they waltzed their way to one of the beds. Max ripped down the spread and stretched her out on the sheets. Her breasts aching from his rough-and-tender kisses, Cassie felt wet, damp heat gush between her thighs, and reached for him.

"Hold on a sec."

He backed away and went for the shaving kit.

"Max!" Groaning, Cassie raised up on one elbow. "Don't shave now. I can take the bristles."

"Shave, hell."

He rooted around inside the kit and dug out a fistful of shrink-wrapped condoms.

"Ya gotta love those Special Forces," he said with a wicked glint in his eyes. "No oiled rice paper or pig's bladder sheath for them."

Laughing, Cassie fell back on the sheets. "Or us, apparently."

"Or us."

He ripped one of the packages open with strong, white teeth and rolled on the condom. When he joined Cassie on the narrow bed, she welcomed him joyously into her body and her heart.

They went through half of Jake Tyler's private stash before rejoining the team.

Showered, shaved and looking very pleased with himself, Max ushered Cassie into the conference room at exactly fifteen hundred hours. She sported freshly washed hair and one heck of a whisker burn on her throat. She covered it up by burying her chin in the cowl-neck of her sweater.

When she entered the conference room, her eyes went instantly to the digitized image projected on the wall-size screen.

"It fits!"

There was their piece, connecting to those brought back by previous Time Raiders. Altogether, they constituted a third of the medallion.

Eight pieces yet to find, Cassie thought with a rush of excitement. Who would go look for them? What time period would they land in?

Eager to hear whether Professor Carswell had deciphered the code embedded in the fourth piece, she dropped into the seat reserved for her. Max took the one beside her. At General Ashton's nod, one of the techs switched on a digital voice synthesizer.

"We'll start with your report. Give us the highlights. You can dictate a more detailed one later."

Cassie took the lead. Succinctly, she related the key events from their landing at the Great Wall to their frantic rush to escape being entombed with the terra-cotta warriors. Max downplayed her description of how he'd saved the empress from a razor-tipped arrow, choosing instead to credit Cassie's psychic ability to sense the weather as the key factor in the success of their quest.

"What about Centaurians?" the general asked when they'd finished their report. "Did you encounter any?"

"None that identified themselves as such," Cassie replied. "But…"

"There was one," Max said flatly when she hesitated. "A palace eunuch who tried to put his hands on Cassie in a way no eunuch should want to."

As embarrassing as it was to admit, Cassie felt compelled to relate how Tai had seemed to invade her mind as well as her body.

"There appears to be a lot of that going around," General Ashton said dryly when she finished. "Tess Marconi said it happened just like that with Lord Rustam. And I, ah, had a somewhat similar experience."

Cassie jolted upright. "Omigod! The Centaurians are here? In Flagstaff?"

"One of them is," the general drawled, "in the shape of my swishy neighbor. I've been waiting to confront him until you two were safely back."

Her voice took on a hard edge. Her blue eyes glittered.

"Tonight, ladies and gentlemen, Allen Parker's alter ego is going down."

Epilogue

It was a battle of epic proportions. Kentar came to it unprepared but fueled by rage.

His command center had just advised him that they'd failed to make contact with Hunter Third Rank Taikin after repeated attempts. The possibility that another piece of the medallion might have slipped through his fingers infuriated Kentar to such an extent that the coarse hair at the base of his neck bristled and his blood ran hot with the primal urge to dominate and subdue all rivals. Beginning with Beverly Ashton. He'd toyed with her—and she with him!—long enough.

She met him at the door, invited him in. His blood was up, his sex heavy between his legs. With an arrogant smile, he threw off the absurd persona he'd assumed.

"I am Kentar of the Fifth Nebula, leader of all Centaurians. And you," he said, his eyes ravaging her, "are mine to do with as I will."

"In your dreams, pal."

Nostrils flaring, he concentrated his force and hurled it at her. She staggered, hit by the dark, undulating waves. Then, incredibly, she turned them back at him.

No! Not her, but the star navigator who emerged from the other room. Small and slender, she didn't look powerful enough to bend a reed. Yet she deflected every sizzling bolt Kentar threw at her. Like lightning gone wild, the crackling energy ricocheted off the walls, sparked across the ceiling, lit the window with brilliant blue light.

He couldn't bend her, couldn't defeat her. Her power was as great as his, made even more immutable by the indomitable strength of Beverly Ashton. "Who are you?" he raged.

"Athena Carswell. Feeling the heat, Kentar of the Fifth Nebula?"

"No!"

"You will."

She smiled sweetly and dropped her gaze to his groin. Her brown eyes lit up like twin lasers.

Kentar's force shattered into a thousand fragments. With a startled cry, he clapped a hand to his burning genitals. The humiliating agony told him he had to get out of there before these two females had him writhing on the floor.

With an immense effort, he gathered his ragged force and willed himself away from this accursed planet. As the earth body he'd assumed began to disintegrate, he locked eyes with Beverly Ashton.

"This isn't over between us. I tell you now,

you and the professor will never find the rest of the medallion."

"Wanna bet?"

Her taunting reply followed him across the vastness of the universe.

* * * * *

*Celebrate 60 years of pure reading
pleasure with Harlequin®!
Just in time for the holidays,
Silhouette Special Edition®
is proud to present*
New York Times *bestselling author
Kathleen Eagle's*
ONE COWBOY, ONE CHRISTMAS.

Rodeo rider Zach Beaudry was a
travelin' man—until he broke down in
middle-of-nowhere South Dakota during a deep freeze. That's when an angel
came to his rescue….

"Don't die on me. Come on, Zel. You know how much I love you, girl. You're all I've got. Don't do this to me here. Not *now*."

But Zelda had quit on him, and Zach Beaudry had no one to blame but himself. He'd taken his sweet time hitting the road, and then miscalculated a shortcut. For all he knew he was a hundred miles from gas. But even if they were sitting next to a pump, the ten dollars he had in his pocket wouldn't get him out of South Dakota, which was not where he wanted to be right now. Not even his beloved pickup truck, Zelda, could get him much of anywhere on fumes. He was sitting out in the cold in the middle of nowhere. And getting colder.

He shifted the pickup into Neutral and pulled hard on the steering wheel, using the downhill slope to get her off the blacktop and into the roadside grass, where she shuddered to a standstill. He stroked the padded dash. "You'll be safe here."

But Zach would not. It was getting dark, and it was already too damn cold for his cowboy ass. Zach's battered body was a barometer, and he was feeling South Dakota, big-time. He'd have given his right arm to be climbing into a hotel hot tub instead of a brutal blast of north wind. The right was his free arm anyway. Damn thing had lost altitude, touched some part of the bull and caused him a scoreless ride last time out.

It wasn't scoring him a ride this night, either. A carload of teenagers whizzed by, topping off the insult by laying on the horn as they passed him. It was at least twenty minutes before another vehicle came along. He stepped out and waved both arms this time, damn near getting himself killed. Whatever happened to *do unto others?* In places like this, decent people didn't leave each other stranded in the cold.

His face was feeling stiff, and he figured he'd better start walking before his toes went numb. He struck out for a distant yard light, the only sign of human habitation in sight. He couldn't tell how distant, but he knew he'd be hurting by the time he got there, and he was counting on some kindly old man to be answering the door. No shame among the lame.

It wasn't like Zach was fresh off the operating table—it had been a few months since his last round of repairs—but he hadn't given himself enough time. He'd lopped a couple of weeks off the near end of the doc's estimated recovery time, rigged up a brace, done some heavy-duty taping and climbed onto another bull. Hung in there for five seconds—four seconds past feeling the pop in his hip and three seconds short of the buzzer.

He could still feel the pain shooting down his leg with every step. Only, this time he had to pick the damn thing up, swing it forward and drop it down again on his own.

Pride be damned, he just hoped *somebody* would be answering the door at the end of the road. The light in the front window was a good sign.

The four steps to the covered porch might as well have been four hundred, and he was looking to climb them with a lead weight chained to his left leg. His eyes were just as screwed-up as his hip. Big black spots danced around with tiny red flashers, and he couldn't tell what was real and what wasn't. He stumbled over some shrubbery, steadied himself on the porch railing and peered between vertical slats.

There in the front window stood a spruce tree with a silver star affixed to the top.

Zach was pretty sure the red sparks were all in his head, but the white lights twinkling by the hundreds throughout the huge tree, those were real. He wasn't too sure about the woman hanging the shiny balls. Most of her hair was caught up on her head and fastened in a curly clump, but the light captured by the escaped bits crowned her with a golden halo. Her face was a soft shadow, her body a willowy silhouette beneath a long white gown. If this was where the mind ran off to when cold started shutting down the rest of the body, then Zach's final worldly thought was, *This ain't such a bad way to go.*

If she would just turn to the window, he could die looking into the eyes of a Christmas angel.

* * * * *

Could this woman from Zach's past
get the lonesome cowboy to come in
from the cold...for good?
Look for
ONE COWBOY, ONE CHRISTMAS
by Kathleen Eagle.
Available December 2009 from
Silhouette Special Edition®.

* * * * *

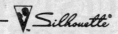

REQUEST YOUR FREE BOOKS!

2 FREE NOVELS PLUS 2 FREE GIFTS!

Dramatic and Sensual Tales of Paranormal Romance.

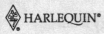

nocturne™

COMING NEXT MONTH
Available November 24, 2009

#77 HOLIDAY WITH A VAMPIRE III •
Linda Winstead Jones, Lisa Childs and Bonnie Vanak
For those who like their holidays with a little more bite,
these are three Christmas tales that are sure to please. In
"Sundown," vampire and bar-owner Abby Brown has grown
accustomed to turning down the advances of Leo Stryker—
a sexy, but human, cop. But when a case puts his life on the
line, she realizes she can't imagine a Christmas without him.

Holidays have always sucked for Sienna Briggs, but in
"Nothing Says Christmas Like a Vampire" that takes on a
whole new meaning when she is saved by the mysterious
Julian Vossimer.

In "Unwrapped," vampire Adrian Thorne comes face-to-face
with Sarah Roberts, the werewolf he had forsaken his clan
for…and the one who had left him to die. Now, during the
season of forgiveness, they find themselves fighting on the
same side again….

#78 DREAM STALKER • Jenna Kernan
Native American healer Michaela Proud thinks her
escalating nightmares signal madness, but the truth is far
worse: her dreams are real. Stalked by the ruler of ghosts,
the only thing standing between her and death is a savagely
beautiful shape-shifter, Sebastian. But can she accept the
man…and the beast?

SNCNMBPA1109